MW01515962

KATHERINE WATSON

Beware the Iron Road

Copyright © 2023 by Katherine Watson

All rights reserved. No part of this publication may be reproduced, stored or transmitted in any form or by any means, electronic, mechanical, photocopying, recording, scanning, or otherwise without written permission from the publisher. It is illegal to copy this book, post it to a website, or distribute it by any other means without permission.

This novel is entirely a work of fiction. The names, characters and incidents portrayed in it are the work of the author's imagination. Any resemblance to actual persons, living or dead, events or localities is entirely coincidental.

This book may contain excerpts of song lyrics for the purpose of commentary, criticism, education, and/or research and is intended to comply with the principles of fair use under copyright law. The inclusion of these lyrics is not meant to imply endorsement, association, or sponsorship by the copyright holders.

First edition

This book was professionally typeset on Reedsy.
Find out more at reedsy.com

to all the little girls who made potions with pine needles during recess.

"Don't let it fool you."

- "Roslyn", Bon Iver & St Vincent,
The Twilight Saga: New Moon,
2009

Contents

Trigger Warnings

Chronic illness

Chronic pain

Self-hatred

Disordered eating

the playlist

AUTUMN
Chapter 1: *Woodland* (The Paper Kites)
Chapter 2: *To Watch the World Spin Without You* (Mon Rovîa)
Chapter 3: *treehouse* (kelseydog)
Chapter 4: *Interlude: I'm Not Angry Anymore* (Paramore)
Chapter 5: *Haunted (Taylor's Version)* (Taylor Swift)
Chapter 6: *Soapy Water* (Chase Petra)
Chapter 7: *I heard you were looking like the moon* (Richard Orofino)
Chapter 8: *Razorblade* (Richard Orofino)
Chapter 9: *Satellite Heart* (Anya Marina)
Chapter 10: *Four Seasons - Autumn in F Major, RV. 293: III. Allegro* (Antonio Vivaldi)

WINTER
Chapter 1: *Tenenbaum* (The Paper Kites)
Chapter 2: *Motion Sickness* (Phoebe Bridgers)
Chapter 3: *It's Alright* (Mother Mother)
Chapter 4: *Keep Yourself Warm* (Frightened Rabbit)
Chapter 5: *Just A Little While* (The 502s)
Chapter 6: *She* (Dodie)
Chapter 7: *Loverboy* (A-Wall)
Chapter 8: *Sweater Weather* (The Neighbourhood)

v

I

Autumn

1

Woodland

"Are you sure you want to get out here, miss? There's... well, there's not much out here."

Carsen smiled at the cab driver. "This is perfect. Thank you so much!"

The man maintained his skeptical expression as he helped her get her luggage out of the trunk and still wore it as Carsen waved him away with a nervous grin. She waited until he had retreated fully from view before she retrieved the letter from her coat pocket.

Miss Cromwell,

I am writing to offer you the position of instructor for our young Maddie. This position is unpaid but offers accommodation, food, and the materials you requested. I trust you and I will come to be great friends, and I look forward to working with you, learning from you, and teaching you what I can.

We'll look forward to receiving you on September 30th,
  Atticus Hastings

Carsen folded the letter and returned it to her coat pocket, sighed, and heaved the trunk out of the mud pile it had been sinking into. Levitating the trunk absently, she began the slow walk into the woods. It was farther than she expected, and by the time she made it to the overgrown railroad, she was limping a bit. She stopped for a moment to adjust her glasses to sit better on her nose, standing next to the tracks and rolling her hips back into place.

The railroad was old, older than most of the town she had just passed through. It looked like it was a part of the ground itself, with ivy growing across it, twisting and turning into patterns that looked almost like cursive. The iron railway was beautiful, but something about it sent a deep chill through her. It felt like the metal path knew she shouldn't be there and was waiting for her to move along, and so she did.

She continued through the woods, stopping occasionally to catch her breath or to pop a joint in and out. By the time she hit the dirt road, she was exhausted. The levitating trunk, which had started above her head, had made its slow way down and now was floating somewhere around her ankles. Every few steps, it would bump against the ground, and she would be reminded to float it a little higher.

When she saw the house, she caught her breath. Everything about it was striking: how the woods cloaked it just so, the friendly curl of smoke coming from the chimney, the

4

ivy growing, the garden. Most enchanting of all was the woman standing out front, looking to be about the same age as Carsen's twenty-two years. She beamed at her from across the yard and started moving towards her at a swifter pace than Carsen would've thought possible. She was big, taller, and broader than Carsen, with copper skin and a square jaw. Two intricate dark brown braids hung down her back. As they met in the center of the yard, Carsen was pulled into a hug, and even though she had never seen this woman before, she felt somehow safe and warm.

"You must be Carsen! I feel like I've known you forever from how much Atticus has been talking about you. I'm Frankie. I live here too. I'm so excited to have another girl around! It's been just the boys and the kids for so long. I was getting so lonely. Do you need help with your trunk? Did you really carry that huge thing all this way by yourself?" Frankie said all of this without stopping for breath.

Carsen took a moment to marvel at the physical specimen of her before she answered. "Actually, I'd love some help. I've been floating it since the main road, but it is getting kinda heavy-" As she finished saying the word heavy, Frankie lifted the whole trunk with one arm and tucked it under her right arm.

"No problem! Let's go inside. I bet everyone else wants to meet you just as badly as I do. They're inside, but I couldn't wait for you to come inside. Sorry about that, but it worked out, didn't it? Cause now I can carry your trunk, and you can have a bit of a break."

5

Carsen blinked slowly, desperately trying to process all of this. Frankie was a force of nature, and she had spoken more words in the last two minutes than Carsen had heard in the last two days. She followed Frankie, who was effortlessly trotting ahead with her trunk, feeling a combination of bewildered, bemused, and incredibly impressed.

They came in through a hallway that could, with a good helping of generosity, be referred to as a foyer. Carsen placed her boots neatly next to the shoe avalanche by the door and went through the doorway to a kitchen.

It felt like the grandmother's kitchen in every fairy tale she'd ever read, small and cozy and warm and well-lit. There was a strong smell of vanilla and apples and stacks of hand-labeled preserves lining the wall next to the wood-burning stove. Frankie grinned easily at her, still holding the trunk like it was nothing more than a feather.

"Awesome, right? I do most of the cooking around here, but these jams are all Fiona. You'll have to ask her about them-it's just amazing the combinations she makes. She grows it all in her garden out front. She comes up with these pairings that you think are going to be absolutely disgusting but end up tasting like they're from some sort of gourmet restaurant. I wasn't super sure about letting a six-year-old loose in the kitchen, but Atticus helps her cut things, and she just does the rest herself."

Carsen, by this point, was admittedly only half-listening. She was walking the permitter of the kitchen, drinking everything

6

in. There was a whiteboard stuck to the fridge. Notes like "Blood delivery Friday!! Don't forget- KEATON THIS MEANS YOU" and "need more ketchup" had been written in a messy scrawl. Drawings of trees and strange abstract shapes lined the board, clearly done by two different children.

A calendar covered in writing hung next to the doorway. The day that Carsen knew to be this month's full moon had "TOTM" written and circled in purple pen. The whole place felt incredibly lived in. Like a place where you could do anything, say anything, and it would be encouraged. Carsen thought fleetingly of her childhood home, which had sometimes felt more like a museum than a house, and felt a warmth spread to the tip of her toes.

"I know Atticus wants to see you right away, but I can show you your room first. We have to drop your trunk off anyway," Frankie said.

Carsen swallowed hard. She hadn't expected to meet Atticus quite so quickly, and to be honest, she was a little scared of him. He had been nothing but cordial in their correspondence, but something about the weight of every single one of his words made her nervous. She'd never taught magick to anyone before, and she'd certainly never worked with children. The last thing she wanted to do was disappoint him. "Okay. Yeah, sure, let's do that first."

She followed the twin pair of braids down a long hallway, with two doors on either side and then a door at the very end.

"This one is yours," Frankie said, coming to a stop. "Keaton is right next door, and I'm directly across the hall next to the girls. Atticus is that big room at the end of the hallway." She kicked open Carsen's door, her boot lining up with a significant scuff that indicated she did this often, and gently dropped the trunk inside. It was a relatively spare room, with just a bed, a desk, a bookshelf, and a dresser. It was, however, a brilliant shade of yellow. Carsen looked forward to inspecting the room in more detail later, but for now, it was evident that Frankie was anxious to keep things moving.

"Alright. Ready to meet Atticus?"

Knowing this wasn't really a question, Carsen simply nodded and followed Frankie back down to the kitchen. They went down a hallway that she hadn't noticed before, one that was dark and smelled a bit like mildew. She made a mental note to clean that as soon as possible. It wasn't necessarily part of her job description as a witch/teacher/medical experiment, but she had always enjoyed cleaning. It kept her calm.

Suddenly, she slammed straight into someone. Frankie snatched her before she could hit the ground and somehow managed to steady the man she had run into at the same time.

"Oh! I'm so sorry. I should look where I'm going. Are you alright?" Carsen could hear herself babbling but couldn't stop. She was transfixed by the man who stood in front of her.

He was pale as porcelain and a reedy thing. Slightly shorter than Frankie, while somehow seeming taller than the both of them. It was something about the point of his chin and the angle of his cheekbones. He looked down at her, and his blue eyes were ice. She felt suddenly and quite acutely that he did not want her there.

"It's fine. Just watch where you're going." His voice was a low rolling twang, a touch of Southern that someone kept despite their best efforts to get rid of it.

And then he was gone, striding off in the opposite direction as fast as his legs would carry him. Carsen felt like a child who'd been caught with their hand in the cookie jar, but she wasn't quite sure why. She turned to Frankie, head cocked in question, to see her rolling her eyes and sticking her tongue out at the man's back.

"Don't mind Keaton. He's a bit shy. Give him a few days, and he'll stop being so grumpy."

Before Carsen could ask any of the thousand questions she had ("That's the other vampire, right?" "He looks like he's our age, is he really only in his twenties? Why does he seem so angry?"), a warm voice called out from just down the hall, beyond the ajar door, beckoning her to come in. Startled, she once again looked at the other woman, feeling a bit embarrassed. She wasn't usually this much of a lost puppy type, but something about this place made her feel off her footing.

Frankie smiled reassuringly at her. "Good luck! I'll see you soon."

9

Carsen watched the braids retreat down the hallway, attached to a woman who seemed a force of nature. She knew she wanted to get to know Frankie, but first, there was business to attend to.

She opened the door.

2

To Watch the World Spin Around

C arsen made her way inside, gaping at the book-shelves that lined Atticus Hastings' office. The shelves occasionally creaked under the weight, and sheets of scrap paper were littered around, sticking out of books, stacked on top of spines. It was the most perfect room she'd ever seen.

There were easily a thousand books in the room, maybe more. Some were standard mass-market paperbacks, and some looked like they were older than the United States. One shelf was exclusively books in other languages; she could see Spanish, French, Arabic, Mandarin, and Russian. There were a few for which she didn't even recognize the writing system. *Surely he's not fluent in all of these*, Carsen thought to herself, marveling. Then again, she reasoned, if you were an immortal vampire, you would have quite a lot of time to study. She wondered absently what Keaton did to occupy his eternal half-life.

"Welcome to our humble home, Miss Cromwell. I hope it's to your liking?" Atticus spoke with clipped vowels in a distinctly not American accent. He was exactly what she had expected - quite tall, with a dark head of hair. His eyes were an odd gray color, and his jawline was broad. He was really very handsome, with that depth beyond his gaze that spoke of many years under his belt.

"Carsen, please. And yes, it's lovely! How long have you been here?"

Atticus shuffled some papers unnecessarily. "Six years or so."

"It's beautiful. So many trees!"

He smiled wryly. "Yes, well, some of our residents prefer the shade. Myself included."

"Oh, right. Of course," Carsen said. An image of a puff of smoke flew through her head, and she shook it away hurriedly. Atticus gazed steadily at her, and she felt in the pit of her stomach that he knew exactly what she'd been thinking about. She had come into this less prepared than she had wanted to - knowing that Atticus was a vampire and that he had been alive a long time was not nearly enough information to get by on. She had a feeling she would have her foot in her mouth more than a few times in the next few weeks.

"Additionally, my daughter Fiona is a dryad, so keeping her among trees keeps her as happy as possible." Another tidbit of news she hadn't expected. She kept her mouth shut this time.

12

Clearing his throat, he gestured to the beaten-up armchair that sat across from his desk. "Please do sit down. We have much to discuss."

She sat, focusing hard on keeping her hands from their typical nervous activities.

"Now, as you know, we hired you because one of my daughters has started to exhibit some... abilities." Atticus looked up at her from his desk, and Carsen was struck by how old his eyes looked. The rest of him gave the impression that he was a dad at a PTA meeting, all of 25 years old, but something about the darkness of his eyes said he'd been around much longer. She must've been distracted for longer than she thought because suddenly, he was clearing his throat and smiling kindly at her.

"Oh! Yes, sorry. Maddie, isn't it? I read the papers you sent. When did you start noticing signs?"

"About four months ago," he answered. "It was just little things at first - she started having nightmares. I thought it was just a bit of growing pains, but then she started predicting things and levitating fruit, and I couldn't ignore it any longer."

"Levitating?" Carsen inquired, impressed. "That's pretty advanced magick for someone with no training."

"It was just a few blueberries at a time, but it was definitely startling to find first thing in the morning," he said wryly. "Once she realized it was a bit out of the ordinary, she stopped doing it in front of us, but when she has nightmares, I go in,

13

and things are floating around, even as she's asleep. I'm quite certain that there are more skills developing that I don't know about. I've asked her, but she won't talk about it. I think she's scared herself a bit, to be honest."

Carsen chewed on her lip, wondering how to ask her question delicately. "Is it alright if I… How exactly did she come to be in your home? What happened to her family?"

Atticus drummed his long fingers on his desk, which was beautiful, a gigantic mahogany thing pockmarked with age and polished to a sheen. He looked slightly uncomfortable, and Carsen almost regretted asking, but she needed to know.

"She came from a werewolf pack that lived just outside the town you drove through on the way here. There was…an incident and a hunting party killed her parents. A contact I have in Bridgeville reached out and encouraged me to take custody of Maddie. That was about four years ago, and I formally adopted her six months ago. Frankie used to live in town, but when Maddie moved in after losing her parents, she offered to come live here and help Maddie adjust to things. The werewolf equivalent of what you're doing, I suppose."

Storing this information about Frankie away, she nodded and smiled. "Congratulations on the adoption!" Carsen's voice came out louder than she had expected in her nervousness, and she winced, but Atticus merely smiled at her.

"Thank you. I had never expected to be any sort of father figure, but both Maddie and Fiona are the best things to happen to me in my nearly 200 years."

Just a look around the office proved this to be true. Pictures of the young girls smiling together were hung all over the office, interspersed with photos of all five of them beaming at one another or mid-play. There was one of all of them in front of a beautifully decorated Christmas tree (that was outside and still in the ground for some reason) on Atticus's desk. Carsen couldn't help but smile. As intimidating as Atticus was, he was also clearly a softie deep down.

She cleared her throat, refocusing. "What is it exactly that you would like me to do for Maddie while I'm here?"

"Just give her some direction. Provide her with the skills to do self-study as she gets older, and teach her that her magick is nothing to be afraid of. Be a sort of mentor. A tall order, I know, but I'm sure you're more than up to the task."

Carsen put on her most confident smile. *I sure hope so.*

—

Carsen's evening consisted of organizing her meager possessions. There were sweaters, yarn, knitting needles, and whatever toiletries had been sat out on her bathroom counter when she was leaving. It was mostly magick books, some newer ones that she'd been meaning to read and some older ones that her mother had given her. She hadn't grabbed much on her way out. *Ugh.* Carsen flopped onto the bed, assaulted with the memory of her way out - the fight with her mother about leaving home, the things she'd said. She'd agonized over it the whole train ride to Ohio. There'd only been a break when she'd gotten there and Frankie had given her the tour around the house.

Frankie, too, was someone she couldn't stop thinking about. Her tawny skin and amber eyes loped through her mind. Keaton sometimes was next to her, his blue eyes judgemental, as though he knew she wasn't meant to be there.

Blinking away the thoughts of the two strapping monsters in rooms on either side of her, she turned her attention to worrying about the thing that had truly brought her here - the promise of a cure. The magickal autoimmune disease that had been eating her as long as she could remember, striking pain into each of her joints and exhausting her from even the simplest spell, was a burden she was tired of carrying. She had found Atticus on an online forum for magickal creatures, and though he responded irregularly, he had just enough medical and magickal know-how to have a shot at curing her. As a medical doctor and a nearly two-hundred-year-old vampire, he had studied magickal illnesses extensively, and it gave her an aching amount of hope that he would have an answer. Though she was excited to be teaching young Maddie the ways of the craft, it was really a fringe benefit, an exchange of her labor for Atticus's. She had put all her eggs into this basket, burning bridges and leaving a life behind to be here.

Carsen didn't know if she could bear it if this too turned out to be a painful and pointless exploit.

She spent most of the night staring up at the popcorn ceiling above her.

–

Breakfast the next morning came with a beginning to Atticus's experiments on her.

"Keaton, why don't you go for a walk? It's lovely outside today, don't you think?" Atticus's tone was at once intensely intentional and flippant, going for casual and landing deep in left field.

Carsen looked up from her tea and toast, eyebrows raised. She shot a glance at Frankie across the table, looking for some sign of recognition, but saw confusion mirrored on her face.

Keaton stared hard at Atticus, then stiffly, as though trying to act but doing it very badly, said, "Yes, I think I will. I love the way that the trees look this time of year. Frankie, you should come with me." He sounded painfully staged. Carsen wondered what Atticus had told him.

Squinting suspiciously at him, Frankie rose from her seat and made for the door, only looking back at Carsen once. "Sure, why not?"

Keaton made to stand up but seemed to get stuck halfway through. He gazed at her, seemingly about to say something. He opened and closed his mouth a few times.

17

"Keaton?" Atticus inquired, looking irritated.

The blond shoved back from the table and was out the door before Carsen had rediscovered the ability to shut her own gaping mouth.

Atticus only let maybe a few seconds pass before he illuminated the purpose of the ruse.

"Carsen, if it's okay with you, I'll take your blood today. Just so I can start working on things."

Oh.

"Alright." Carsen stood up, slightly embarrassed. The search for a cure for her bones shifting and popping and her healing at a snail's pace had been going on since childhood. She had seen dozens of doctors, and they'd all said the same thing. *It's incurable. Grin and bear the pain. It'll never go away. Goodbye, and good luck.* Her mother hadn't given up, had insisted she see all the doctors she selected for her, even long after Carsen had accepted her fate.

Atticus opened the door to his office for her, and she stepped in, feeling even more unsettled than she had the first time she'd done this. He had a small silver table out, smelling sterile and with several vials and needles organized neatly on top. It was achingly familiar to her.

"Are you comfortable with the sight of blood?" he asked calmly, indicating to the seat that was clearly intended for her.

18

"Shouldn't I be asking you that?" she joked.

Atticus didn't laugh.

Carsen swallowed hard. "Yes, I'm fine with blood." She'd had her veins blown enough times to have no real feeling about the process anymore.

"Good. I'll need to take a fair amount, so I'll bring you some juice when I'm done, just to balance everything back out. No strenuous exercise for the rest of the day."

She was quiet as he placed the needle, watching as his practiced hands popped vials on and off as the needle yielded a steady drip. She wished she could see into the liquid, look at the atoms and find the mistake that left her like this.

"Why did Keaton have to leave for this? You can't even smell the blood, it's not being exposed to the air."

Atticus smiled wryly. "You might not be able to, but we can. We can smell it when it's still in your veins - it leaving is almost painfully strong."

Carsen tipped her head back in the chair and closed her eyes, pushing away the guilt of making her host uncomfortable. "How can you bear it, then?"

"Plenty of practice."

—

19

Atticus made her stay seated for twenty minutes, sipping apple juice and eating chocolate cookies, and feeling sorry for herself. When she finally was permitted to leave, she carefully pushed herself up and thanked him for his help.

The moment she shut the door to his office and leaned against it, sagging bonelessly as her eyes closed. She'd been here less than a day and was already so tired it felt like the crushing fatigue was eating her insides.

"Carsen?"

She startled, opening her eyes.

Keaton was sat at the foot of the stairs just outside Atticus's office door, looking a little lost. His eyebrows were the most expressive part of his face, and right now they were furrowed together so tightly that they looked like a single brow.

"Keaton?" She answered, imitating his tone almost unconsciously.

"Atticus has a habit of making promises he can't keep," Keaton said, fingers tracing the hollows of the wooden staircase.

Carsen wanted to sit down next to him, ask him what he meant, to have their first real discussion. However, she knew that sitting down on those stairs would mean getting back up again, and that would mean her knees popping out of place, and that would mean making that inevitable and terrible noise of pain, and then she would embarrass herself in front of this man who already thought so little of her. So she stood and went on to wonder if the conversation would have gone differently if she hadn't.

"What is that supposed to mean?" she asked.

"It means what it means," he offered obtusely.

"Well, that's helpful." She was going for light and breezy, but it didn't come out that way, and his eyes were shuttering, and he was standing, and she knew she had fucked up.

"Wait, I-"

"I just wanted you to know what you were getting into." He turned and started up the stairs.

"Dinner is at 5:30, you two," Frankie's voice rang out from the kitchen.

"I'm not hungry, thank you." Keaton didn't even slow his pace.

Frankie was next to her now, hands clenching and releasing over and over again. Carsen realized too late about the supernatural hearing that werewolves were endowed with. Frankie had, without a doubt, heard the whole thing.

"Are you alright?" She asked.

"He hates me. I don't know what I did in the singular day that I've been here, but he does. It's like my very existence

21

is offensive to him." Carsen was careful not to let her voice break, but it had a strain in it that was embarrassing to her.

"Every rose has its thorns, I guess[1]," Frankie said quietly, watching Keaton's back retreat.

There was something in her tone that made Carsen turn to look at her just in time to see a softness in her eyes spark and fade. Frankie was watching him go like it was the only thing that mattered, exuding a perpetual certainty that he would be back despite any evidence to the contrary.

So it's like that, then, Carsen thought, trying not to be disappointed but finding herself that way nevertheless. She was disconcerted to find that she wasn't sure which of her two new housemates she was disappointed about.

3

Treehouse

Carsen's night was sleepless, but the morning was beautiful. Birds were chirping pleasantly in the trees, leaves were falling, and the smell of autumn permeated all the way through the walls of their house. If there was a candle that smelled like that morning, Carsen would buy every single one. She got dressed before making her way to the kitchen, not feeling quite comfortable making a public showing in her old sweatpants and t-shirt. The hallway smelled like bacon and coffee, and her stomach grumbled. She had begged out of dinner the night before, wanting to have a tiny bit of time to settle herself, and now she regretted it.

The kitchen was filled to the brim with people. Frankie was flitting about between the stove, where eggs were frying next to a pan full of bacon, and the coffee maker. Atticus and Keaton sat together at the kitchen table, serenely sharing a teapot. Two cups steamed. As Carsen got closer, she saw that there was blood inside, red and smelling strongly of iron. She did her best to give no indication that she did not typically dine with people who took their morning blood in fine china.

"Good morning, Carsen. Did you sleep well?" Atticus was cordial, sipping from his cup with a pinky finger extended. Keaton gazed impassively at her from the table. He had self-consciously put down his cup and instead was gnawing at a piece of bacon like his life depended on it.

"Carsen!" Frankie's enthusiasm rolled off of her in waves. "Do you like coffee? Eggs? I can make you toast if you want."

"Give her a second to wake up, Franks." Keaton had moved from the bacon to his eggs now, still avoiding his cup of blood.

"I love coffee," Carsen replied, moving towards the pot. As she did so, she examined the kitchen a little more closely. There was a sign on the wall next to the sink, and she read it with a smile on her face.

HOUSE RULES:
  - all plants must stay OUTSIDE
  - no silver
  - move pencils with care!!
  - use your inside voices & kind words
  - knock first!!

The conversation between the other three had abruptly stopped when Carsen had entered, so she drank her coffee in awkward silence, shuddering to think how loud her swallows must be to the super-powered ears in the room. She finished the cup quickly and stood.

"Where would I find Maddie?" Carsen asked.

"I expect she's in the tree house. It's a bit into the woods. Go past the old weeping willow. Maddie should be expecting you, and I told her to mind you, so do let me know if she misbehaves." Atticus smiled encouragingly at her.

Carsen gave an awkward nod before heading for the woods. She wasn't walking for too long, just long enough to pass several trees with deep gouges in them, scratch marks it seemed, before she came upon the fort. "DO NOT ENTER" was written on the doorway[2] in a childish scrawl. The wood was warped with time and water, but the fort looked cozy nonetheless.

The sounds of a soft conversation carried down from inside. *They must both be in there.* She edged a little closer, and the two young voices became clear.

"Do you think she'll be nice?"

"I don't know. I hope so."

"What if she's a mean witch? Like in the stories Atticus reads to us?"

"Not all witches are mean." The voice sounded indignant and a little hurt, and Carsen gathered that this must be Maddie. Feeling a bit guilty about eavesdropping, she knocked gently

25

on the door. The voices quieted, she heard frantic low whispering, and then the door swung open to reveal two little girls. One was tall and thin, the other very small.

"I'm Maddie," the tall one said solemnly, sticking out a thin hand to shake. Doing her best not to laugh at how strange the formal gesture felt taking place in a child's tree house, Carsen took it and shook.

"It's a pleasure to meet you, Maddie. I'm Carsen." She turned to the other girl. "So you must be Fiona then."

"Yup!" The little girl popped the 'p' with her lips, and Carsen grinned at her. This would be fun.

They were the reverse of what she had expected. Maddie was dark and willowy, her nose just that bit too long and too sharp for her small face, the type that you grow into as you get older. She looked at home among the trees, what Carsen had imagined a dryad would look like. Not at all the traditional image of a werewolf.

The actual dryad, Fiona, looked more like one of the cherubic small children from a hot chocolate commercial. Her cheeks were round and rosy and her blonde hair was curled into two tangled buns at either side of her head. Carsen immediately adored both of them.

"Would you like to have class in here today?" Maddie seemed hesitant at the thought of this, so Carsen quickly added, "Only if you'd like to, of course."

26

Maddie stared at her, face utterly still. She seemed to be deciding something.

"Alright. Come in. Fiona, I'll see you later."

Fiona bounced away, the curt dismissal clearly not perturbing her in any way. Carsen stepped inside the fort.

–

Carsen was on top of the world after their lesson. Maddie seemed to have taken to her at least decently well and had the makings of a powerful witch. She'd never met a werewolf before, but it seemed to be some sort of magnifier for her magick. Carsen certainly hadn't been able to produce a full windstorm in her first class. She made a note to ask Atticus if he had a copy of *Blood, Bones, and Magick: Genealogy and Witchcraft* in that library of his, having read it ages ago and holding a vague memory of some mention of a vampire who had been a witch before she'd turned. She was deep in thought, trying to come up with any other books that might help, when she came around the corner to Atticus's office and pulled up short. Two raised male voices came from within.

"What were you thinking bringing her here?"

4

Interlude: I'm Not Angry Anymore

This was not what she had been hoping to have happen during her first week. Feeling only a little badly about it, Carsen quietly slid up to the door, casting a sound-enhancing spell as she did.

"What were you thinking?" The voice said again, and now that she was closer, she recognized it as Keaton's low and slightly twangy grumble. "Bringing a human here? A *human*?" The disdain in his voice made Carsen's spine straighten a bit. "With Maddie on the verge of the change and the full moon right around the corner? How could you be so irresponsible?"

Carsen was shocked to hear this level of one, genuine distaste and anger that she was here, and two, disrespect for Atticus. Not only had Keaton struck her as someone who would be polite even if it cost him something, but Atticus seemed to be a *presence* in this house. She had felt it the moment she stepped inside. He wasn't the sun or the earth, nothing that dramatic, but he was the gravity, the magnetism holding this house together. Keaton's voice was sharp and firm, and she was almost impressed at the bravery it must've taken to say these things. Even if he was saying them a little loudly and rudely for her taste.

"Do you think that I brought her here without thought? That I would ever willingly put any of you in danger?" Atticus's staccato speech felt even shorter when juxtaposed closely with Keaton's broad vowels. "I knew you didn't have the best opinion of me, Keaton, but this is truly something else."

"What about *her*? She's in danger simply being here. And what about the kids? Did you think about them, Atticus? If one of them does something, how are they supposed to live with that guilt?"

Carsen knew that she should step away, pretend she hadn't heard any of this, but her curiosity kept her rooted to her spot. She had accepted the post with limited knowledge of what was to come, in an admitted fit of foolhardiness, and truly hadn't thought about any potential danger in working with young magical creatures. It wouldn't be the worst thing in the world for her to get some perspective, even if she had to eavesdrop with a bit of magick to get it.

"Are you afraid for the kids, Keaton? Because I think you might be worried for someone else." Atticus's voice was cold, and she knew immediately that she never wanted to hear that tone directed her way.

She had already quickly lost her place in the conversation,

29

which she knew vaguely she should have been offended by. Angry footfalls started their way towards the door, with not nearly enough notice for Carsen to get on her way and pretend she hadn't been listening. Seeing no other option, she stood fast in front of the door and prepared herself for a confrontation.

The door flew open at about the same pace that Keaton's jaw did when he saw her outside. Carsen had really hoped to be friends with him, but given what she'd just heard, it was seeming more and more like that wasn't going to be possible. So why not go all in?

"Do you have a problem with me? Have I offended you in some way?" She heard her own voice, sharp and a bit squeaky, and wished that she could, for once in her life, summon even the tiniest bit of gravitas.

Keaton looked appalled by the question, looking to Atticus, who stood behind him for help. When he found none there, just a slightly smug face, he turned to her, lips pressed tightly together. "I don't have a *problem* with you. I just don't think you should be here." He said this as if it made nothing but perfect sense and that she might be an idiot for not coming to the conclusion herself.

Carsen couldn't believe his gall. She scoffed. "Do you see why some would categorize that as a problem?"

"Listen, I'm not sure you understand the situation you've been brought into. There are monsters living in this house. Me,

30

for instance. I could tear you apart if I wanted to, do you understand that?" he raged, stepping closer to her, clearly trying to use his height and growling timbre to impress upon her the danger that she was in.

Carsen, who hated more than anything else being told what was and was not in her best interest, didn't give a shit.

"Well, do you want to?" Her voice was calm, which seemed to make Keaton even angrier.

"Do I want to what?"

"Tear me apart. As you so artfully put it."

"Of course not!" He looked offended at the prospect as though he hadn't been the one to bring it up.

"Then what's the problem?" she demanded.

Atticus stepped between them. "I think it would be best for everyone if we all took a step back and gathered ourselves." This was directed almost entirely at Keaton, and Atticus was gazing at him with a look that seemed almost fatherly. Dimly, Carsen wondered how often he had to give that look to Maddie and Fiona to have so artfully perfected it.

Keaton, surprisingly, seemed mollified by this enough to take a step back from Carsen, looking a little abashed at his sorry attempt at intimidation. His anger at Atticus didn't seem to have waned, though, and he turned to glare at him.

"I hope you don't regret this." Keaton spat at Atticus before turning on his heel and storming away.

Carsen watched his back as he left, wondering how hunger worked for vampires. The very vaguest of outlines of Keaton's ribs were showing through the thin, long sleeves he was wearing, and she felt a pang of something she couldn't identify. Rather than try, she turned to Atticus, who looked deeply disconcerted. It made her uncomfortable. She shifted from foot to foot nervously, the floor making a creak that summoned Atticus from his reverie.

"Perhaps you should come in." He held the office door open for her.

—

It was strange to see Atticus so clearly unsure of what to say next. She had sat in the same chair she had taken the day before and waited for him to speak, but he hadn't, opting instead to stare into space, contemplating something beyond her comprehension. Finally, she had to break the silence, if only for her own sanity.

"Is everything alright?" Carsen asked hesitantly.

"Yes, it will be. There's a lot of history there," Atticus murmured, looking absently at the door. "And I've made a lot of mistakes." Shaking his head to clear it, he turned to look at Carsen and smiled a bit. "Would you like to see?"

Carsen raised her eyebrows. "What do you mean?"

32

Atticus smiled a bit, looking more at ease now that he was in a professorial role. "Have you spent much time around vampires?"

An odd question but one she took in stride. "No. You all are the first magickal creatures I've met. Besides me and my family, of course, but I don't suppose we count."

Atticus generously did not confirm the obvious, that yes, witches did not come even close to the level of magick and power coursing through this house on the daily.

"We vampires have a unique power over the mind, you know. We can read each other's thoughts. A bit irritating at times, but very convenient. Different vampires have different specialized skills, but Keaton and I have both been blessed by the most common one. We have the ability to share a memory, with only a touch."

Carsen clicked her jaw shut to keep from gaping at him. "Huh," she said vaguely.

"So rather than tell you the whole sordid tale, which would take ages and would be tainted by my point of view, I can simply show you what's happened. No need for speech and no risk of editorializing. So, I ask again... Would you like to see?"

She only hesitated for a second.

"Yes."

He beamed at her. "Excellent." He reached out and grabbed her hand, and they were gone.

–

"I was born in 1824 in a small seaside town in Scotland." Atticus's voice was all-encompassing and comforting, like being wrapped in a weighted blanket. She saw the ocean and felt the cold, salty wind on her cheeks. She also saw a small boy, dark-haired and innocent-looking, running along the rocky beach with a handmade kite.

"I had every bit the typical upbringing of an upper-middle-class boy at that time, sent away to boarding school at Fettes College, then onto university. It was there that I fell into trouble."

The scene changed and she was in what she somehow instinctively knew to be Edinburgh, Scotland's present-day capital. A young Atticus, not more than a teenager but getting close to it, was carousing down the stone-paved street with a pack of other boys, yelling and shoving at each other.

"We were charmed by our own vulgarity, enchanted by our unruliness. It was everything we weren't supposed to be, in total opposition to the upstanding young men that we were expected to play. I'm ashamed to admit that I did many things that I'm not proud of. "

It got very dark very quickly, and young Atticus was striding through an alleyway, the moon lighting his path. A beautiful redhead walked beside him, laughing at something he had

34

said. He smiled, pleased with himself.

"I did whatever I wanted, whenever I wanted. I went to places that I had been told were not for the likes of me, and I enjoyed every moment of it. Until the last moment."

There was a blur of movement, and for a split second, Atticus was obscured, and then he was on the ground, his neck a gruesome bloodied piece of meat rather than resembling any sort of body part. The woman was gone, leaving a high, cruel laugh in her wake.

"I suppose I got what I deserved. I don't remember much from my turning, just the briefest scent of perfume. It was agonizing, those first few days, while I became what I am now. When I woke up, I was profoundly changed. Not just in what my appetite preferred but in who I was. A trial by fire had been good for me."

"After a few decades passed, I had recovered my control enough to be among humans again. I finished my studies in medicine at the University of Edinburgh under a different name. It was such a spectacular time in that field, with new things happening all the time. Joseph Lister was one of my attendings as I did my clinicals. I stayed around as long as I could until people started to notice that I wasn't aging."

Carsen stared at where Atticus still lay wriggling desperately on the ground, too staggered for speech. Almost as though he sensed her discomfort, the scene changed. Atticus was walking through the moors, the mist resting on his cold skin.

35

He looked utterly alone.

"I spent a few decades crisscrossing the United Kingdom and then came to the States in 1907. More than a million people did that year, so I blended in. I was just like all the rest of them, looking to start a new life in the promised land. It was very hard to hide what I was in Scotland. Very small, with not a lot of people, and plenty of insular towns where people do little else but talk. America was a sweeping empty landscape, and more importantly for a vampire, it felt utterly lawless."

Images of Ellis Island danced in her head. The streets of New York, cobblestoned and full of people from all over the world. Atticus, looking more hopeful than he had in the last scene. Carsen felt her mouth curve up in a place far away from her.

"I flitted about for many years before I found a friend in Keaton."

Images started flying through her head, an out-of-control stream of consciousness that left her feeling wind-blown and motion-sick.

Keaton, eyes blazing and broken, begging, "I need your help."

Atticus's steady reply of "I'll do what I can."

Suddenly, Carsen was back on the beat-up chair across the table from Atticus, eyes wide. "What happened?" she demanded, without preface.

"I've told you all I can. The rest of the story isn't mine to share. I'm sorry you had to see that. This thought-sharing is a funny thing."

Her glasses had slid down her nose, and she left them down long enough to look over them, appraising him. This was, without a doubt, one of the strangest conversations she'd ever had. He held up under her gaze, though, and she let the question go unanswered for now.

"Thank you for sharing that with me. It was very... illuminating." Carsen was starting to think more and more about the fact that she was living among beings that had been alive for decades and decades longer than her. As she passed Atticus to leave, she tried to ignore the way that her spine stiffened involuntarily. The way that it would around a predator.

‒

"I'll be going to the mailbox later this morning if anybody has anything they want to send." Atticus said this while looking what felt pointedly at her, so Carsen said "If you could, I'd like to write a note back home," and dutifully went to get a piece of paper from her trunk.

She stared at the blank page, feeling pretty blank herself. She had hundreds of things to say when she lay in bed at night. What are you supposed to say after fighting with your mother and then leaving before you have a chance to apologize? *I don't think badly of you*[3]. *I miss you every moment, but I don't know if it's enough to come home for.* After a few minutes, she

37

shook herself. *This shouldn't be so hard. Just say something. Anything!*

Hands shaking only a bit, crying only a little, she uncapped her pen.

Hi Mom,
   All is fine here. The girls are very sweet, and Maddie is already excellent at elemental work. Hope you're well.

Love,
   Carsen

She trudged back downstairs and handed it to Atticus without comment. The room was thick with tension. Keaton and Frankie were both avoiding eye contact, Frankie uncharacteristically silent. Atticus was staring devoutly at the kitchen table, which felt somehow worse than if he had said something. She muttered something about going to her room and spun on her heel, knowing that she was pouting like one of the girls might but not able to bring herself to care. She regretted it the moment she handed Atticus the letter, thinking of all the things she should've said, wishing she had said nothing at all.

She spent the rest of the day lying in her twin bed, alternating between drowsing, pondering, reading, and the occasional scream into her pillow.

5

Haunted

Weeks passed, and fall deepened, the leaves falling to the ground slowly and then all at once. The girls delighted in crunching them thoroughly under their feet, jumping in leaf piles as fast as Frankie could rake them.

Carsen woke one morning to find the trees all empty and everyone abuzz at the breakfast table.

"We're going into town today!" Frankie announced excitedly, holding Maddie's sweater aloft as she beamed at the rest of them. "It's brisk out today, so wear something warm for the walk."

Walk? Carsen crossed and uncrossed her legs, staring at the table. "Fun! How far is the walk, exactly?" Atticus looked up sharply at the concern in her tone, clearly realizing what she was really asking.

"It's about a mile each way. I'm sorry, Carsen, I hadn't thought-" Frankie started.

"It's fine!" Carsen interrupted, trying her best for a bright tone. She paused to steel herself for what was to come in light of her next sentence before adding, "I'll just bring my cane."

Keaton and Frankie looked at each other with raised eyebrows in a way that they clearly thought was subtle but couldn't have been farther from it. Maddie schooled her expression into something resembling uninterested (evidently, she had been briefed on proper etiquette for this sort of thing). Atticus looked regretful. It was only Fiona, who was still just a bit too young to have a complete grasp on tact and all that came with it, who asked, "What's wrong with you?"

Atticus closed his eyes as though in prayer. "Fiona, we don't ask people 'what's wrong with them.' Please apologize to Carsen."

"No, no, it's okay! Really." Carsen had expected far worse and was honestly glad that someone had said something. In her experience, it was more uncomfortable when it sat and festered and was a forever undertone in the way that people looked at you. Answer the question outright, and it could just become another fact, like the fact that her eyes were green or that she was short.

"My magick is a little broken, so it makes things a bit harder sometimes. I use a cane to help me for longer walks and things like that." The simplistic explanation was enough for the girls, but she knew that it wouldn't be enough to satisfy Frankie and Keaton, not forever. Atticus already knew but was too polite to tell either of them anything explicit without her express permission. In the first few days, she had mulled over possibly having him tell them for her. Sometimes, you could get away with never having to talk about it. However, something about Frankie's face made her want to tell her. Keaton, on the other hand, could think what he wanted, but Carsen didn't plan on baring her soul to him any time soon.

She busied herself with pouring another cup of tea, allowing them to digest this information without an audience. By the time she had added her mugwort and maple syrup, they seemed to have properly processed the news, so she looked up from her mug. Keaton was pretending to wash a dish in the sink. Maddie and Fiona looked studiously at the table. Frankie and Atticus were having some sort of conversation with their eyes that she couldn't quite grasp. Carsen cleared her throat.

"But it's fine, really. A walk sounds lovely." She paused to watch Keaton scrub his perfectly clean plate. Doubtlessly he was thinking about how not only was there a weak human in their midst, but a broken human no less.

"Should we get ready to leave then?" Atticus said, sounding the slightest bit strained.

Keaton suddenly dropped the dish and turned towards the rest of them once again, face as impassive as ever. "Yes, I think that would be best. It'll get dark at six, so you should come

41

back home as soon as you can," he said.

"Are you not coming?" Carsen asked, cocking her head. They had all been pent up in the house since she'd gotten there, and she had assumed that Keaton would take the first chance he got to get some space from the rest of them.

"Someone has to stay with Fiona," he said shortly. "She can't go that far from her tree."

Shit. Carsen had an abstract concept of dryads but clearly not enough of one. She looked sideways at Fiona, hoping she hadn't upset her. Fiona, though, looked unperturbed and simply requested that someone buy her sugar so she could try and make a maple apple tart with her most recent harvest.

The next twenty minutes passed in a flurry of last-minute grocery store requests and looking for missing shoes. By the time they were on their way, Keaton was looking thoroughly sour, and Carsen was quite glad to be giving him run of the house by himself for a few hours. Maybe he'd be in a better mood when they got back.

–

Atticus walked a bit ahead of them, holding Maddie's hand and pointing out different flora and fauna, using each one's scientific name to describe it. The distance between them seemed tactfully designed to allow Frankie and Carsen the privacy to talk, and Carsen appreciated it.

"Are you alright? You don't have to talk about it if you don't want to, but if you d,o I can-"

"It's okay, I want to tell you," Carsen interrupted her, sensing the beginning of a typically Frankie-length monologue in the air.

They walked quietly for a minute, just the sounds of leaves crunching and the faraway voices of Atticus and Maddie talking about types of mushrooms. There was no point in mincing words. She would find out anyway.

"My magick is eating my bone marrow. Every time I cast a spell it takes a little more from me. It's just going to keep getting worse, and I'm on a timeline." She let that piece of information sit out in the open between them. It was heavy in the air, and she couldn't make herself look over and see how Frankie was taking the news. She didn't expect that Frankie would like her back even before this information was provided to her, but in her experience, nothing hampered romantic attraction like the news that your prospective partner had a range of mobility similar to someone three times their age.

"Actually, in addition to tutoring Maddie, while I'm here I'm going to work with Atticus a bit to see if there's any sort of medication he can come up with. I read about his work with Joseph Lister back in the day, and my hope was that with my experience with herbal medicine and his grasp of science, something could come of it."

She hadn't realized that she was nervously yanking at her fingers until Frankie slipped hers through them. Her hands

43

were rough and warm, and Carsen could feel the ridges of the scars lining them. She looked over to see Frankie looking at her steadfast, perfectly calm.

"Atticus is a genius. He'd never say it, but it's true. He'll come up with something." She sounded absolutely certain in a way that Carsen didn't think she'd ever been about anything before. The tightness in her shoulders eased.

"I hope so," Carsen said. She squeezed Frankie's hand.

Frankie squeezed back.

—

As they walked past the Bridgeville welcome sign, Atticus, a bit twitchy, mentioned he had someone to meet, reminded them to reconvene at the usual place, and walked quickly in the direction of the town's singular coffee shop. Maddie had been talking about wanting to read one of the new Ron Robinson books so Frankie, hand still intertwined with Carsen, directed them towards the library. Their talk in the woods had loosened something between them, and Carsen could feel the stars in her eyes when she looked at Frankie becoming more and more pronounced.

When they got to the library, a crumbling brick building that looked like it was just about the oldest standing piece of architecture in town, it was closed, so they decided to do their grocery run while they had the chance. Everything seemed to be going fine; they had picked up the sugar Fiona had requested and the matcha for the foul tea that Atticus insisted on drinking every morning. It was only when they got to the toiletries section that the problem arose.

"Oh, tampons! That reminds me, Maddie, have you thought about whether you wanted to use tampons or pads? It's getting to be time for us to start thinking about that." Frankie was completely nonchalant, throwing a box of tampons in for herself. The calm tone the conversation had started with made the turn all the more shocking.

Maddie immediately began to cry, great wracking sobs that shook her thin frame in a way that was frightening.

"Maddie!" Frankie sounded as surprised as Carsen felt. "What's wrong? It's perfectly fine if you want to start out with pads-"

"Nothing. Nothing is wrong. I'm going to go get some cereal." Still taking heaving breaths, Maddie was halfway to the next aisle before Frankie and Carsen had collected themselves enough to look puzzled.

"What on earth was that about?" Carsen had finally regained her voice and did her best to subtly peer after Maddie, who was moving so fast her red sweater was practically blurred.

"I have absolutely no idea. I've never seen her like that before. Ever. It has to be about her period, right? Should we talk to her about it?"

"I don't know. I think maybe we should let her come to us."

Carsen felt woefully underprepared for this whole situation and was more relieved than an adult ought to be when Frankie nodded her agreement.

"Okay. We'll wait. But we should go find her now. I don't want her to be alone and upset in a supermarket."

When they recovered her near the oatmeal, Maddie was completely composed and carried on a conversation about the merits of steel cut versus rolled oats as though nothing had happened. Following her lead, they checked out and walked back to the library, carrying on banal conversation. When they arrived, the closed sign was still showing in the window, and all three were prepared to give it up as a bad job when they heard a breathless greeting from down the street.

A tall woman with cheekbones so angular she looked nearly cat-like was striding towards them, straightening her messy hair as she beamed at her latest patrons.

"I'm Zahra! You must be Carsen. I've heard all about you. I'm the librarian here," the woman said in rapid-fire fashion. "Frankie, Maddie, how are you? Here, let's get inside. Maddie, I've got that book you were asking about last time. "

Her dark skin nearly glowed from the inside out, and her brown eyes somehow looked golden in the sun. *Does everyone in this zip code have to be so gorgeous?* Carsen thought, self-consciously shoving her glasses up her nose.

–

46

By the time they had found everything they were looking for it was close to four o'clock. The three of them said a hurried goodbye to Zahra and rushed to the butcher shop. Atticus picked up a supply of blood for him and Keaton there every week and was sitting outside on a bench with three large paper bags at his feet. He stood as they approached, already asking about the books they'd checked out from the library.

Maddie eagerly answered, but Carsen was staring at the dark lipstick smeared against his neck. She turned to look questioningly at Frankie, but she was busy pretending to be interested in a flyer in the nearest shop window.

"Oh wait! Atticus, you have marker on your neck. How did that get there?" Maddie sounded astounded at Atticus and his absent-mindedness. Frankie made an awkward coughing sound, her fist barely covering her smirk.

"Thank you for letting me know, Maddie." Atticus rubbed at it with a handkerchief, not making eye contact with either of the women. Carsen was quite certain he was thanking his lucky stars that vampires couldn't blush too much.

–

When they got home, Carsen hightailed it to the kitchen, hoping to get her willow bark pain salve and get out before anyone caught her. No such luck. She had just released a deeply embarrassing whine of pain, reaching for the jar when a low, rolling southern accent came from behind her.

"Let me get that for you," Keaton said.

Internally, Carsen cursed wildly, creating compound words that were previously unknown to the English language. On the outside, though, she smiled.

"That would be very kind of you."

In the last few days, she had resolved to try harder to be friends with Keaton. The house was a very small place to have an enemy, and surely he was a perfectly nice man who just happened to have a resting bitch face. It seemed like she was being proven right when her acceptance of the offer of help garnered a slight smile from Keaton. The first show of softness she'd seen from him in the last two weeks. He slid in next to her and pulled the jar down with ease. It was the closest she had been to him, ever, and she was struck by how *human* he smelled. Like sweat and fresh laundry and boy. She had vaguely expected vampires to smell like dust and mothballs. So far, everything she had expected about all of this had been completely and utterly incorrect.

He handed it to her, still offering the smallest of smiles. "Did you enjoy your trip into town?"

Carsen grasped onto this show of friendliness like it was a lifeline, and she was drowning. "Yes! Yes, it was very nice. The librarian was lovely, and the supermarket had pumpkins we could carve later this month. I'd be happy to stay with Fiona next time so you can get a chance to get out of the house."

His smile had taken on a strange frozen appearance, but for the life of her, she couldn't imagine why. "That's alright, I don't mind." He was already turning inward again, turning from her and edging towards the door. There was a fragile line[4] she could always feel herself walking when they spoke, and she could never tell when she would cross it until it had already happened.

"Still, you must get cooped up staying here all the time. It would be no problem to-"

"No, thank you," he said abruptly. "You'll have to excuse me."

He was gone before she could say anything else, leaving the room cold and Carsen pondering how many more mysteries this house could possibly hold.

6

Sparks Fly

ine. That's just fine. If Keaton wanted to be weird and cagey about every little thing, who was she to stop him? She'd done her part. He could do and say whatever he wanted, and she wouldn't care, not one bit.

Heart aching for no particular reason, Carsen limped her way back to her room, clutching the salve like the liquid gold that it was. She had perfected the willow bark formula after what must have been a thousand tries, and it worked better than even she had hoped it would. The only problem was that it had to be applied directly to the area of concern. When mobility was already an issue, the bending and twisting involved in the application was the last thing she wanted to be doing. The payout, in the end, was worth it, but the process itself was agonizing.

She shut the door as quietly as possible, hoping that everyone else was either outside, too deeply engaged in their own activities to notice her, or an asshole who hated her for no reason. Stripping down to her bra and underwear, she screwed open the lid and spent a moment simply breathing in the reassuring minty smell. She started at her shoulders, then went to her wrists, saving her hips and ankles, the more difficult spots, for last.

As she expected, when she reached for her hip, there was a stabbing pain, as though someone had inserted a hot poker right into the center of it. She didn't anticipate the loud groan of pain that escaped her. And she certainly didn't expect to see Frankie ram her way through the door, looking concerned.

Today was officially the worst day ever.

"Oh, my God? Oh. Oh, shit. Carsen, I'm so sorry, I thought you had hurt yourself. I-" She was turned halfway around, with her fingers covering most of her eyes. Not all, though. Clearly, she wasn't yet convinced that Carsen *hadn't* somehow managed to injure herself sitting still on a bed.

"It's okay! It's okay. I'm sorry I disturbed you, I was trying to be quiet. I was just putting on a medicinal salve." Suddenly, she realized how illicit the whole affair was looking, her in her undergarments, hands slick, fingers on her waist, groaning. Carsen prayed that her cheeks weren't as blazing red as she thought they were, but a cursory look up at the mirror on her vanity told her there was no such luck. Definitely the worst day ever.

Frankie said nothing for a moment. She had given up pretending that she wasn't looking at her and was now unashamedly staring at her, at her body. It was a unique sensation for Carsen, who had spent her entire life hiding from the unfortunate fact of her physical form, both from the way it looked and the pain it caused her. An odd stirring was in Carsen's stomach when she asked, "Could you maybe... help me?"

She didn't know what came over her and would have regretted it the second it left her lips if Frankie hadn't given such an enthusiastic chirpy "Of course!"

She shimmied onto the bed, her umber skin looking ever so striking against Carsen's white duvet. "So what do I do?"

That was an excellent question. "So I still have to put it on my hips and ankles... If you're comfortable with it... Um... Could you...Uh..." She was waffling as she had never before. Frankie gingerly slipped her fingers beneath the waistband of her underwear and carefully smoothed the salve onto her skin, following the ridges of her right hipbone.

Perhaps not the *worst* day ever.

"You're good at that." Carsen's voice was ragged and shy, and she barely recognized it.

"Well, I have a fair amount of experience with injuries - part of the werewolf territory." She ruefully pushed up the sleeve of the flannel she was wearing over her flowered dress to reveal what must've been a hundred bite marks lining her bicep.

52

Carsen felt the air whoosh out of her. "Can I?"

Frankie took her hand and guided it to her arm. The bites were raised, some more than others, some thicker than others. It felt like she imagined a book of braille would be under her fingers. Carsen ran her fingers, wondering what story each ridge of skin told.

She was struck with the urge to pull her fingers away, but she kept them pressed there. Carsen recognized this exchange of vulnerability for what it was, and there was no way she was going to ruin it.

"Do they hurt?" Looking closer, she could see the deep scratches interspersed with the puncture wounds from a powerful jaw. Most of the arm was scar tissue, some of it raised and some of it sunken, all of it soft under her fingers. Carsen absently wondered what kind of moisturizer she used to achieve this kind of softness before returning to the matter at hand.

"Not right now," Frankie said, sounding purposefully careless. "They did when I got them, obviously. And when the full moon gets closer, they get a bit sore." She had moved on to Carsen's ankles by now, circling the joint over and over again with her thumb. "Most of the time, it's just a dull ache."

"I could probably make something to help with that." Carsen bit her lip, praying she hadn't overstepped.

Frankie was quiet a moment, and Carsen was sure that she

had fucked everything up irrevocably. Then Frankie looked up from the bedspread at Carsen, revealing the most tender look she'd ever seen on anyone's face.

"Do you mean it?"

"Of course I mean it. I want to help."

Tears were starting to shine a bit in Frankie's eyes, so Carsen looked away, telling herself it was for Frankie's privacy and not to ease the sadness in her stomach.

"Are you hungry? I think dinner is soon. What do you like?" Frankie changed the subject, voice impressively clear and steady.

"I'm not really hungry right now," Carsen answered, grimacing a bit as she shifted on the bed. The analgesic was starting to kick in, and now that the pain was lessening, she could pay a bit more attention to the overwhelming sense of fatigue that was encompassing her.

"Oh. Okay." She so clearly wanted to help, and Carsen felt like an asshole for turning her down.

"Actually, if it's not too much trouble, I wouldn't mind having a little something. I just don't know if I can get up right now," Carsen said honestly.

The way Frankie's face lit up let her know she'd made the right decision.

"Well, I'll just bring it to you! Like breakfast in bed. But not. Because it's not breakfast. You know what I mean."

She bounded off for the kitchen without another word, and Carsen felt gratified with the knowledge that at least she could do something the right way with *one* person in this house.

She settled back into the pillows with a sigh. Frankie's movements through the kitchen were audible even through the closed door, and the slight din was a comfortable background noise. She closed her eyes, just for a second.

—

A knock startled her awake.

"Hi! Sorry that took ages. Maddie and Fiona ended up wanting some too, and then Atticus and Keaton did, and before long, I had to make enough for the whole house." Frankie was poking her head through the door, holding two steaming plates of pasta.

Carsen bit back a yawn, shoving herself upright in a desperate attempt to look like she was cool and fun and hadn't fallen asleep at five in the afternoon. "That's okay! Thank you so much for bringing it to me. You didn't have to."

"Of course." Frankie slid the door shut as quietly as she could and edged her way up to the bed. "Sorry if it's a little bland. The recipe calls for garlic, but it makes Atticus and Keaton all itchy, so we don't keep any here." Frances set the plate down in front of her, looking the picture of domestic bliss with her

55

pristine apron and the muscles of her arms pressing against the sleeves of her dress.

"Do you want me to eat with you?" She was still standing next to the bed, holding her own plate and looking uncertain.

Carsen sat up fully and patted the bedspread next to her. "I would love nothing more."

—

The next morning, Carsen rose early, made her tea, and stiffly wobbled out to the back porch, following the sound of chatter. She found Frankie and Keaton sharing a plate of toast and a pot of coffee and Keaton sporting a smile wider than she had yet to see from him.

"Am I interrupting?"

Keaton's smile dropped, but Frankie positively beamed at her. "Here! Come sit next to me. There's some butter left for you to put on your toast."

Moving carefully to avoid disturbing any of her still sore joints, she made her way to the chair next to Frankie.

The three of them sat quietly for a moment, silently appraising one another. Just when Carsen thought she couldn't take it anymore, Keaton's eyes softened, and he pushed a jar of preserves across the table.

"Try some of Fiona's jam. It's cherry and pear. She described it as 'cherry forward'," Keaton informed her, trying to sound sarcastic even as his tone was heavy with affection for the little girl.

Carsen despised cherries. She took the jam, spread it liberally on her toast, and took a huge bite. Her eyes lit up. "Wow. When are we sending her to the culinary institute?"

"Any day now," Keaton said dryly. Frankie took a thumb and wiped the sticky residue from the side of Carsen's mouth.

Conversation flowed freely after that, and Carsen even managed to make Keaton chuckle. It was a low, pretty thing, and the second she heard it, all she wanted to do was hear it again. The morning warmed a bit as the sun rose, and they tired themselves out with talk, finally sitting together in contented silence. A tiny tornado of golden leaves twisted beneath the feet of the table, her joy whipping itself up in the wind. Frankie plucked a leaf from Carsen's tangled hair.

"I'm glad you're here, Carsen," she said.

Carsen grabbed her hand under the table, feeling heat shoot through her. "Me, too."

Keaton almost smiled.

–

"Focus on any anger that you've ever felt, every time that you wanted to cry but held it back," Carsen whispered, eyes on Maddie.

57

They sat together cross-legged in the midst of the forest, Maddie's eyes pressed shut in concentration. Storm magick was on the lesson plan that day, and Carsen was incredibly excited about it. It was her favorite form of magical expression, and she had had a hunch since she arrived that Maddie would be a dab hand at it. She was a stormy little girl, after all, eyes brimming with lightning if she felt she'd been wronged, tears as easy to prompt and as fast to rush as a summer rainstorm.

She was succeeding far beyond Carsen's wildest expectations. The wind was whipping in from the west, tossing her bangs around. The trees shook with the force of the storm that was coming, leaves turned inside out, and branches rattling. Maddie's dark hair remained perfectly in place.

Suddenly, a lightning strike sounded, a few miles away but still close enough to shake the earth. The sky opened up, and water rushed down, soaking them both instantly. Maddie's eyes flew open, and she laughed with delight. Carsen did too.

"Perfect, Maddie, just perfect. It is practically unheard of to summon a full-on rainstorm[5] on your first try. Now, see if you can stop it."

This was the hardest part, damming up the flow of emotion, and it proved just beyond Maddie's ability. The wind slowed a bit, and the thunder dimmed, but the rain kept pouring as steadily as before, maybe even a little harder.

Carsen shrugged. "No matter. We'll work on that next time. You're getting soaked, though. Run!"

Maddie shot to her feet and began running, loping really, at a preternatural pace. It was easy to forget that she was a werewolf, given she hadn't turned yet, but every once in a while, she would have a moment that reminded Carsen irrevocably of Frankie and her amazing strength and speed. Carsen sensed that this was about to be one of those moments.

The little girl turned to run but stopped short and looked back at her teacher. "What about you?"

It was kind of her to ask. The pain hadn't quite dissipated from the previous day, and Carsen had needed her cane to get out here. No, she would not be running alongside Maddie by any stretch of the imagination.

She shrugged at the girl, honest in her indifference. "I love the rain. Don't worry. Go ahead, I know you're freezing!"

The pale face grinned at her, hair soaked and sticking to her cheeks, and started sprinting. It was startling, the speed she achieved within seconds. Carsen allowed herself a moment of wishing for that sort of gift and then struggled to her feet. Gripping her cane for dear life, she began the trek back. When the ache of the pressure change hit, she soothed it with the image of Frankie drying her hair with a towel, a vision she had had earlier that day and held onto as the hours passed.

7

I Heard You Were Looking Like the Moon

September came to a close with a cold snap, and the house woke up to a thick frost coating everything. It looked like the entire world had been crystallized, a beautiful, almost snow globe.

Carsen felt like she was in her own personal fog, though hers wasn't nearly as pretty as the one outside their windows. Atticus's latest effort to cure her, a foul herbal tincture she had to drop on her tongue morning and night, had not only not worked but had left her unable to eat, throwing up even water.

Keaton had been storming around the house since it had started, and she had heard snatches of muttering, things like "Of all the irresponsible..." and "Should have his medical license revoked...". Frankie had been making fresh batches of ginger tea every hour and chattering nervously about anything and everything under the sun, every few hours apologizing profusely for everything as though it was somehow her fault. Atticus was always apologetically insisting that it would go away with time. Carsen was too nauseous to feel any sort of way about any of it, instead opting to remain horizontal until it passed and not think about anything too much.

It was on the third day of this misery when Carsen heard a tiny knock at her bedroom door. Frankie snapped to attention, waking up mid-snore from her nap in the worn armchair next to Carsen's bed.

Carsen, who had been affectionately watching Frankie as she slept, focused very hard on the door as though it had always been the object of her attention. "Come in!" Her voice sounded croaky but better than she had expected, so she took it as a victory.

The door opened a crack to reveal Maddie looking uncomfortable. "Hi. I wanted to...check on you."

Frankie beamed at this. Carsen privately marveled at her ability to be so beautiful and pleasant less than thirty seconds after being in a deep sleep.

"I'm going to get some more ginger tea." The older werewolf stood and practically danced towards the exit. She closed the door behind her, and Carsen returned her focus to Maddie, who was standing next to her bed, looking incredibly uncomfortable.

"I hope you're feeling a little bit better[6]," Maddie said, staring

61

at her shoes. "I miss our classes."

Carsen felt the small hole in her heart start to stitch itself back together again. "I miss them too, Maddie. Actually if you want, I had everything ready for class before I got sick. We could do lessons in bed this week."

Knowing she would regret it later, she wiggled her fingers dramatically at Maddie, and the classroom began to shape itself together; books flying from their places under dirty clothes, pens clattering around in their jar on her desk before creating an airborne pinwheel that spun around Maddie's head.

Carsen and Maddie spent the morning in Carsen's room, the corner of which she had fully transformed into a makeshift classroom, complete with a whiteboard, a stash of pens, and stationary. This week, they were learning about the moon cycle, the moon's magical properties, and all the various rituals and spells that needed to be performed during each stage. Carsen had enlisted Keaton the week prior in drawing a detailed chart of each moon phase, something he achieved in miraculous detail considering his only tool was a dry-erase marker.

It was turning out that the whole house was full of strange and wonderful talents - she had known to ask Keaton because she had accidentally stumbled across his canvas and paints in the storage shed out back. He did beautiful landscapes, and when she came to ask him, he acted appropriately humble, but she could tell he was quite proud of them. He had every right to be - the skylines of New York City were easily recognizable, his rendition of the California redwoods was breathtaking, and the watercolor of the Mississippi River made her feel like she was there.

So, teacher and student sat in Carsen's room, discussing the difference between a harvest moon and a hunter's moon.

–

It was coming to be that hour between evening and nightfall, and the sun had started to set. To a backdrop of beautiful blues and spectacular pinks, Atticus and Carsen walked (Atticus walked, Carsen limped, leaning heavily on her cane) the perimeter of the house, discussing Maddie's progress. The haze of nausea had lifted, and she was finally able to brag about her student the way she deserved to be bragged about. She'd come a long way in only a month, and Carsen was half considering making a report card for her, if only so that Atticus could hang it up on the fridge.

A murder of five crows was pecking at the ground near the back porch as they made their third loop.

"And I think that a big part of the reason that she's improving so quickly is due to her being a werewolf. She has this sense of herself, this orientation in her own mind and understanding of her place in the world, and that is a tremendous help, especially when doing elemental work. I know I didn't do half the things that she's managed until I was thirteen at least. She's a marvel, really."

Atticus beamed at this. "I've certainly noticed an improvement in her mood. I think having someone around who understands has been a great help to her. I can't thank you enough for that."

Carsen felt a deep sense of pride well up through her stomach and fought the urge to get teary-eyed. "Thank you. I'm glad that I can be of help here."

"How are you settling in? I've noticed you and Frankie seem to have become...fast friends." The implication was clear, but Carsen didn't have time to respond and possibly tell him it was none of his business because suddenly there was a yell from the woods, just beyond their view.

"Frankie!" The cry came from a little into the woods, and Atticus and Carsen flew toward it. Keaton stood panting, looking shell-shocked, staring out into the woods beyond and looking even more deathly pale than usual.

"What is it, what's happened?" Atticus's voice was sharp, and he was looking around wildly.

Carsen was staring at the ground. "Is that hers?" she asked quietly. She pointed at the
   puddle of blood on the dirt floor, soaking into it and making a maroon mud that sent a chill down her spine.

"Yes," Keaton confirmed. "She changed, and I think she wasn't expecting it. It's earlier in the day than usual, and she startled and started scratching at everything, including herself, and then she ran. That way." Keaton pointed west.

The three adults looked at one another for a split second, and then Carsen made up her mind. "I'm going to go look for her."

"No, you aren't." Keaton's tone was sharp, and he glowered at her as though she had brutally insulted his mother. "Are you really that crazy?"

"She's hurt!" Carsen had already decided and was already moving towards in the direction Keaton had pointed. She stopped short when Keaton grabbed her arm.

"You can't go by yourself. I'll come with you," he said grudgingly.

Atticus looked between the two of them and where Maddie and Fiona were playing, clearly wanting to help but also needing to stay near the girls.

"Okay. You can come." This was all a terrible waste of time, and Carsen was antsy to get going. "But we need to go now. Atticus, someone should stay with the girls, right?" She added the second part to give him the out to watch the girls that he was so clearly looking for, and he took it.

"Yes, I'll stay with Fiona and Maddie. If you're not back in a half hour, I'll come looking."

"Fine. Come on, Keaton." Hands shaking with adrenaline, Carsen forged her way deeper into the woods.

They walked through the woods, calling out for Frankie. "Will she remember her name?" Carsen asked suddenly, realizing the potential futility of their actions.

"She will. She's in there, and she's fully aware." Keaton was walking even slower than her despite his longer legs and her leaning on her cane, and she resisted the urge to yell at him to hurry up.

"Why would she run like that? Does she usually do that?" Carsen was doing her best to scan the forest floor and watch for Keaton's reaction at the same time.

"Not usually. Typically, she knows it's coming. Sometimes, when she's upset, though, it happens before she knows it." His voice was dark, and Carsen remembered that they had been alone together before it had happened. She wanted to ask if they had been fighting but was distracted by a trail of broken branches and leaves spotted with blood.

"Look! She must have come this way."

There was a sudden whining coming from the dark just beyond them, and the pair looked at each other frantically. Keaton must have been more worried than she had realized since he snatched her hand and yanked her along, nearly off her feet.

"Franks? Frankie, it's me, it's Keaton. Are you alright?"

They broke into a clearing to find a gigantic wolf curled up on the forest floor. Carsen sucked in a breath, even as she rushed towards her. The wolf was huge, its tail alone as long as Carsen's entire torso. Its fur was the same dark brown as Frankie's hair, and when Carsen kneeled down next to the wolf and saw her open her eyes, she saw the same welcoming amber color she melted in on Frankie every time she looked at her.

Frankie gave a high-pitched heartbreaking whine, and Carsen felt like her veins were iron, like she was magnetized to stay with her, like she would be violating her own polarization by leaving her.

"What did you do to yourself?" Keaton murmured, running his cold hands gently along her front legs. He must've hit a wound because the wolf yelped and shied away. "Sorry, sorry, I'm sorry." He held his hands up in surrender, looking helplessly at Carsen.

"What's the plan here?" As soon as Keaton asked, Carsen realized that this was as far as she had thought ahead. She couldn't let him know that, though. Instead, she turned to talk to Frankie.

"Can you walk, sweetheart?" It was an overly familiar endearment, but the occasion called for it. The wolf let out a harumph that seemed to be affirmative, and tentatively stood, giving a low whine as it did.

Carsen shyly reached out to stroke Frankie's head. It was

silky soft, the undercoat warm and comforting. Frankie, or the wolf, or maybe both (Carsen still wasn't totally sure how this worked) gave a pleased-sounding grumble.

"Let's go," Keaton said stiffly. Carsen turned to look at him, but he was turned away, looking in the direction of where they had come from.

They started back, a slow, strange procession of three. Frankie stood double of Keaton in this form, so Carsen and Keaton stood under her odd shadow in the moonlight.

Keaton stumbled at one point, letting out a yelp oddly similar to the one Frankie had given earlier, and Carsen reached out and steadied him with both hands.

"Are you alright?" She asked, looking worriedly at his face, which was drawn and pale.

"Fine. Let's keep going," he said roughly, pulling his shoulders out of her grasp.

When they reached the house, Atticus was pacing the back porch, eyes a bit wild. As he saw them, his shoulders loosened visibly, even from across the yard, and he started towards them.

"Is everybody alright?" He appraised all three of them with equal interest.

"She's fine. I think she should rest now," Keaton said distantly.

"That sounds like an excellent idea. Frankie, I know you prefer to be outside when you're...like this... but perhaps sleeping in your own bed would do you good," Atticus added.

The wolf harrumphed but leaned its warm weight against Carsen and nodded its furry head. And that's how Carsen came to tuck a giant wolf under a quilt and give it a kiss good night.

–

Frankie came to slowly, eyelids fluttering.

"Hey, you." Carsen smiled tiredly at Frankie. She had spent the night in an uncomfortable chair to watch over the other woman and apparently had fallen asleep because Frankie was back in her human form, and Carsen hadn't seen the transformation. She imagined that was probably for the best.

"Carsen?" She blinked. "Carsen!" She was bolt upright, looking wildly around the room. "Did I scratch you? Bite you?"

She still sounded vaguely feral, and Carsen thought that maybe if she was smarter she would've been scared, but she couldn't quite bring herself to be. "No, no! I'm fine, everybody is fine. We're mostly worried about you."

The werewolf settled back into the bed, eyes still wary, and Carsen subtly took her healing kit out from under the chair she was sitting on. "May I? Some of those scratches are pretty nasty, it'd be good to get them disinfected sooner rather than later."

Frankie nodded silently, so Carsen moved from the chair onto the bed and opened the kit. Carsen ever so gently wiped peroxide on the deep gashes on Frankie's back, letting the wounds fizz before she sprinkled yarrow on them to stop the bleeding. She could feel the werewolf tense under her fingers, but she didn't make a sound.

"Does it hurt?" Carsen kept her voice soft, not sure if the other woman was ready to talk.

Frankie scoffed. "No, the blood is just an aesthetic choice."

Carsen's hand stilled, but before she could pull away, Frankie was turning and grabbing her hands in her own, catching her eyes.

"I'm sorry, I didn't mean that. I'm always grouchy after, but I shouldn't take it out on you. Especially when you're being so good to me."

"I meant, does it hurt now? I can give you something for that," Carsen asked, forcing herself not to have hurt feelings.

"Yes. I'd like that." It was a clipped response, but a response nonetheless, and Carsen felt she might be able to get an answer to her next question.

"Why did you run?" Carsen whispered.

"It scared me. The change, I mean. Normally, I have it planned. I know what's coming and when. But it hurts to change. You feel everything: every bone crack, every nail grow. I panicked." She seemed embarrassed, though Carsen didn't know why. It sounded like a terrifying experience, one she knew she could not undergo nearly half as gracefully as Frankie did.

Carsen wasn't sure what to say, so she said nothing at all, merely finishing cleaning the wounds and then giving her hand a squeeze.

"I'll go get you some of my willow bark salve."

Carsen finished tending to Frankie as fast as possible, given how obvious it was that the other woman wanted to be alone. She returned to her bedroom and shut the door as quietly as she could before sighing and flopping on the bed. *I'll just close my eyes for a little while*, she thought to herself.

She shot up in her bed an unclear amount of time later at the sound of an awkward throat clearing in her doorway.

"Oh, my God," she gasped, clutching her chest.

Keaton stood there, leaning on the doorframe, looking only vaguely apologetic. "Nope, just me. Have you had any water today?" His voice was sentimental, and he looked frustrated by the feeling in it.

Keaton didn't seem like the sort of person who asked if you'd

71

eaten. She doubted that he had done such a thing in years, given how awkward he looked. As if to avoid being exposed for having a heart after all, he swept out of the room.

Carsen could hear him heading for the kitchen. She felt her eyes close again but opened them when she felt a weight on her comforter. This shape felt cooler than Frankie had but just as solid. She opened one eye to find Keaton staring at her.

"I brought you some water since I know you've not been drinking nearly enough. And I know you've not eaten anything today either. Quite irresponsible, actually." He said this all very fast, as though if it came out quick enough, she wouldn't hear the care behind the words.

"Have you been keeping tabs on me, Keaton?" Carsen was embarrassed at how endeared she sounded by the prospect.

"Someone has to," he said shortly, looking away, clearly deeply uncomfortable.

Carsen slowly sipped the water, not breaking eye contact with him. She could see that Keaton was watching the way her throat moved as she swallowed and Carsen tried to not feel self-conscious.

"It was good of you to go after her like that," he said suddenly.

The compliment made Carsen's stomach flip. Keaton's compliment giving was so rare a thing that it could best be described as literally once in a blue moon. To get one from him was to hold liquid gold in your hands. She tugged at a strand of hair that was falling out of the French braid Frankie had done yesterday morning, embarrassed at the flush in her cheeks.

"I didn't want her to be alone out there. It seems... lonely." Carsen watched Keaton's face as she said this, looking for some sort of understanding in it. She had yet to have any real conversation with the man and kept hoping she'd catch something in the corner of his mouth or the tilt of his eyelashes that would explain to her what he was thinking. There was nothing there, no new understanding between them. He simply looked paler than usual.

"Yes, well. Thank you for doing it," he said stiffly. Just as quickly as the crack had opened up, Keaton slammed it shut and moved away from the bed. "I have some things to do," he said over his shoulder.

Carsen stared at the space where Keaton had been standing and wondered if she would ever be able to have a real conversation with him.

–

The day had passed fairly quietly, and before long, they had all made their way to the kitchen table for their evening salon before bed. The grown-ups' talking time could last until 10 PM or until the wee hours of the morning, depending on the topic. When the conversation turned to world politics, Atticus held court at the head of the table while Keaton made arguments pulled from obscure political movements.

In the meantime, Frankie and Carsen played Rock Paper Scissors under the table. When discussing magickal history, Carsen could expound for hours about witch trials and traditional herbal medicine's adaptation to the modern world, while Atticus hummed appreciatively, and Keaton would ask questions, genuinely interested, while Frankie looked on contentedly.

That night they were all quieter than normal, less having a conversation and more sharing a communal space for the sake of being around one another. Frankie and Carsen had been talking softly about Maddie's progress, eagerly going over her successful magick lesson that day. Atticus had his nose in a book that weighed as much as Fiona, and Keaton sat sullenly, looking out the window to the spot where they had seen the crows earlier.

Frankie stood suddenly, looking concerned. "Keaton? What is it, what's wrong?"

Carsen looked up from the sweater she was mending to see Keaton utterly green. Atticus was already moving towards Keaton at warp speed, his face twisted with worry and fear.

"When? How long has it been?" Atticus demanded of Keaton.

Feeling as though she had missed something big, Carsen stood too. She didn't move closer, instead letting Atticus and Frankie encircle Keaton as she watched. The concerned circle seemed like a place she hadn't earned entry to yet.

"Oh my God, Keaton! Why didn't you tell me?" Frankie was sobbing now, shaking shoulders and quick breathing.

"You didn't mean to." His voice was quiet, his eyes distant.

And then suddenly, with no fanfare, Keaton Beauregard fainted.

8

Razorblade

They all went into motion instantly, Frankie and Atticus grabbing his arms to keep him from falling out of his chair and Carsen instinctively breaching the inner circle to help.

"What happened? What did he mean, 'you didn't mean to'?" Carsen was all professionalism now, reminded of the years she had spent assisting in her mother's apothecary. The man in the chair whimpered, and she checked him for fever more tenderly than she thought was possible. He was lukewarm to her touch, and knowing how cold he usually ran a swooping worry shot through her.

"I must've scratched him when I changed," Frankie said miserably. "It's like an infection to a vampire."

Atticus didn't say anything, just gently rolled up the arms of Keaton's sweater, while Carsen looked over the white forearms. Nothing.

"Take his sweater off, please." Carsen rolled up her own sleeves, thinking about what sort of herb or potion could possibly help with the infection of a vampire's blood. Did vampires even have blood? Surely not, right?

Frankie peeled the sweater off, careful not to jar Keaton as she pulled it over his head. She gasped. A long scratch crossed his torso, the edges of the raw skin a terrible green color. Bubbles were erupting, and a mottled red and green rash was breaking out across his chest, the most disgusting and terrifying Christmas decorations ever seen.

Atticus and Frankie groaned in sympathetic harmony, and it was enough to jar Keaton awake. His eyelids fluttered, and Carsen breathed again.

"Keaton? Keaton, can you hear me?" Her voice sounded more confident than she felt, and she was glad of it. The crumple of Keaton's brow made him look very young, and she wanted to reassure him, even if just a little bit.

"Carsen?" His voice was shaky, his eyes half open. He looked terribly fragile. "What's happening?"

Many things with Keaton were very difficult, but helping him wasn't. "You're hurt, but it's going to be fine. I need you to stay awake, okay? Please don't close your eyes,"[7] she implored, one eye on his perilous hold on the chair and the other on the door to the kitchen. Her herb cabinet seemed a million miles away.

He groaned, slumping further down the seat.

"I'll take that as a yes," Carsen said, looking to a distraught Frankie, who looked frantic and disgusted with herself. "Can you get my bag, please? It's in the front hallway." The other woman tore away like a thing possessed and returned with the bag in hand within seconds. Keaton shifted in his seat, and then cried out, surprising himself and everyone else in the room.

"I know, I know, it's going to be okay," she said soothingly, tearing her eyes from the tincture she'd dug out of her bag and moving to adjust him in the chair. She was unused to touching him, and he was softer than she had expected him to be. Where does it hurt?"

"Everywhere," he moaned.

His pain was like a razorblade pressed against Carsen's veins[8].

Carsen registered that Frankie was backed up against a wall, looking stricken. She needed to find a way to get Frankie out of there, so she wouldn't have to witness what was going to have to happen next.

Time to take charge, Carsen decided. "Okay, here's the plan. Atticus, can you check on the girls? I don't want them to wander in and see something that might scare them. Frankie, I need you to carry Keaton to his bed, and then boil some water for me. I'm going to check my herb cabinet."

Everybody sprung into action, and Carsen watched as Frankie picked Keaton up more gently than she'd ever seen a person do. She was barely even touching him, yet he was completely and totally supported, held like a baby. His head lolled into the crook of her shoulder, and she pressed her cheek against his forehead before straightening up and walking quickly and carefully towards the hallway where their bedrooms were.

–

Holding a whole host of herbs, one for every possible complication, she entered Keaton's room. As she stepped inside, she realized that she had never been in his room. There was a bookshelf almost sagging with magazines, albums, and thick novels. A small collection of masks from Carnaval hung on his wall, staring empty-eyed out at her. Interspersed between the masks were a variety of Mardi Gras beads. In the corner was a cello, polished to a sheen, and standing at attention next to a music stand. Everything about the room revealed a personality and past in Keaton that Carsen had no idea existed, that he simply refused to let her see. She was caught up for a moment in the realization, but a low groan from Keaton reminded her of the job at hand.

Frankie had propped him up in bed, where he was looking a little more with it, albeit still green.

She went for light-hearted. "Well, Frankie, how is our patient doing?"

"He seems a bit better? Maybe?" Frankie answered. She wasn't herself, looking anywhere but at them. She floated from the

79

bed to the cello, plucking the strings, clearly not there, mind a million miles away.

Carsen turned her gaze to Keaton and found that he was also watching Frankie, eyes deeply worried. There was something sweet about it if she wasn't so maddened by the risk he had taken. She was sure she'd come around to appreciate it fully later.

"I'm glad to hear it. Here, drink this, it'll help." She offered him a thermos, lid firmly screwed on. The tea she had concocted would numb the pain for now, but because it looked like mud, she wanted him to drink it as quickly as possible without trying to delay because of the tea's unappetizing look (and smell).

Keaton took it gratefully and took a huge slug, his face screwing up. He had barely swallowed it before making a gagging sound. "Frankie, she's *poisoning* me," he whined.

Frankie gave a weak laugh, evidently unamused and still as far away as she could get in the corner with the cello, fiddling with the tuning pegs.

"It's not poison, drama queen," Carsen said mildly. "It's valerian root and turmeric. It's a sedative, but I enhanced the potency of it. You might be a bit loopy for a while, but it'll hurt less."

He took a deep breath to steel himself, then drained the contents in one impressive gulp. Carsen took the thermos from him, watching closely to make sure he didn't bring it back up. She had before. It really did taste foul and smelled even worse.

"That was, without a doubt, the worst thing I've ever put in my mouth," he announced, swallowing several times to make sure it was entirely down his throat. "Can I have some water?"

Frankie was there holding a glass of water in an instant, still a ghost of herself.

He thanked her and swished it around his mouth, then dramatically gargled it. "Thank you, doctor. I think I may just recover."

He seemed most worried about how Frankie was handling this whole thing, and to be honest, so was Carsen. She turned to the taller woman with an apologetic smile.

"Could you go wait in the hallway for a second, Franks?" Carsen asked. "I'm sorry, I'm just going to be doing some complicated magick, and I need to really concentrate."

"Of course." Frankie practically fled the room, looking grateful for the excuse to be out of their eyesight for a while. Carsen was sure that she would be in tears before the door was closed. She turned her attention back to Keaton on the bed, who was looking at her suspiciously.

"What pray tell 'complicated magick' are you going to be doing on me?" he asked, sounding a bit nervous.

81

She grinned ruefully at him. "It's an old and sacred magick called disinfectant."

"Then why-"

"Even with the tea, it'll hurt. Badly. And I figured you wouldn't want Frankie to see that. I assume that's why you didn't tell anybody about this?" She said this last bit a little scornfully, peering at him over her glasses with barely contained anger (which was probably mostly worry).

He looked abashedly at his hands, twisting his fingers together. "I knew she would be upset. And blame herself, even though it wasn't her fault. I thought I could handle it quietly."

"Our definitions of quiet must be very different." Carsen normally had a much better bedside manner than this, but she felt personally offended that Keaton had put himself in this amount of danger and pain, seemingly on purpose. This was the same man who had been chiding her about drinking water mere hours ago, and here he was, running a weird vampire fever with an infected torso and giving her attitude.

"I know. I know, it was a mistake. But I thought I could keep her from knowing, and that would have been worth it. I'm sorry, I don't always know what's best[9]. But I know you would have done the same." He looked steadily at her, and she felt him looking deep into her soul. He was right. She probably would have if the tables were turned.

"Alright. I'll stop giving you grief, but only till you're better.

Then I get to be mad again."

"Deal," Keaton said with a weak smile.

"Okay. Let's get ready to rumble, kid." She brandished the disinfectant, and he braced himself, gritting his teeth.

–

After she finished cleaning everything, a task that Keaton handled admirably and without so much as a whimper in pain, she called Frankie back in. "You should stay with him tonight, I think," she said to Frankie. "He's going to be perfectly fine, but he'll need someone to keep an eye on him, just in case the fever spikes."

Frankie looked vaguely nauseous. "His fever is going to spike?"

"It won't!" She reaffirmed, kicking herself. "He's going to be perfectly fine. I bet he'll be walking around grouching at us all come morning. It's just a case of better safe than sorry."

She turned to leave but stopped at a quiet voice behind her.

"Thank you." He was mostly asleep, and maybe it was due to that that it was the most sincere she'd ever heard him, and she felt her cheeks warm a bit. She didn't turn around to prevent him from seeing it, merely saying good night and leaving the room.

–

83

"Carsen!" Frankie's voice sounded happy, but Carsen still ran to Keaton's room, tearing open the door.

Keaton sat completely upright, the color back in his cheeks, sipping at a plastic cup with a metal straw in his mouth. She knew it was blood from the way that his cheeks held the smallest tinge of pink. It would only last for about twenty minutes after he drank, but he always looked closest to human in those few moments.

"How are you? Are you in any pain?" She demanded, drawing closer. Frankie sat cross-legged at the foot of his bed, eyes not leaving his, almost as though she couldn't believe this liveliness from a man who twelve hours ago had looked so pale it was deathly. Carsen was similarly impressed. Keaton, despite his immortality, always seemed a bit frail. It was easy to forget that he was fairly invulnerable to most things in this life.

"I feel great. Whatever was in that nasty tea worked a trick."

"So you feel better?" She demanded, stepping a bit closer.

"Like I could run a marathon," he answered, grinning broadly at Frankie.

"Good. So I can do this." She brought herself up to her full height (which if she was being honest wasn't terribly impressive) and summoned every bit of scary witch she could.

"What were you *thinking*?" It came out a squeak, and she

84

pretended that it was just because she had the voice of a chipmunk and not the wave of relief that she was riding.

Keaton raised a single eyebrow almost disdainfully. "Is this the anger I was so nervously waiting for? Remind me to make you angry more often. This is almost fun."

This blasé response left Carsen seeing red. She could feel her hands going numb with magick that was only just contained, and she took a deep, calming breath before speaking in a low quick tone that carried through the room as well as any shout would have.

"You terrified every single one of us. In trying to protect Frankie's feelings, you nearly did yourself serious damage, caused a panic, and upset Frankie terribly. I sincerely hope you never *ever* pull a stunt like this again." All the worry and fear she had been holding in her chest the last few hours came out with a whoosh, and she was more strident than she had ever known herself to be. She couldn't quite bring herself to regret it.

Frankie gave a quick intake of breath at the sharpness in her tone but otherwise gave no indication that she disagreed with Carsen's tirade.

Keaton barely gave a sign that he had heard her, just stared at her steadily, chewing on the inside of his cheek like his life depended on it. Finally, he cleared his throat.

"It won't happen again. I promise. I'm sorry for scaring

everyone."

She was still a bit angry and tempted to decline this olive branch, but in the end her pacifist side won out.

"Alright. Well, if that's all, I think you have some people who'd like to speak with you."

She pointed a finger at the door, and it swung open, revealing Atticus and the girls. She'd had a silencing charm on it to keep them from hearing the argument that she knew was coming, so they had utterly no idea what was going on. Maddie and Fiona ran for Keaton's bed at once, squealing delightedly at this rare opportunity to sit on a big bed rather than the small bunk bed they shared.

"Gentle, girls!" Frankie reminded, moving quickly to ensure that they didn't tackle him.

Atticus looked at Carsen questioningly.

"He'll be fine. Might be a bit tired the next few days, but that's all."

Atticus's shoulders slumped with relief. "Thank you, Carsen."

She smiled at him, then watched as he and Frankie joined the girls on the bed. They all were chattering animatedly, and no one noticed her slip out.

9

Satellite Heart

There was an uncomfortable tension in the house the next few days between Keaton and the rest of them. He was clearly unhappy to have been so publicly vulnerable in such an uncharacteristically dramatic way and was sullen and sulky as a result.

Frankie lost patience with it halfway through the morning when he pretended he didn't hear her ask how he was.

"Really, Keaton? Just because you're embarrassed doesn't mean you have to act like a little kid. You're worse than the girls."

He would have colored at this if he could, but since he was bloodless by definition, he merely said, "I'm doing fine. How are you?" He slid into the spot at the kitchen table next to her and his fingers grazed her shoulder in a soft way that seemed to scream apologetic.

Frankie was as quick to forgive as she was to anger. She immediately launched into a long story about the twists and turns of the dream she had had the night before, as though nothing had happened. Atticus watched all this happen with his typical impassiveness, the only indicator that he noticed the bickering being a knowing look he shared with Carsen over the brim of his teacup.

She still wasn't quite sure how this whole house worked. There were a thousand layers, every shared glance so loaded with meaning and history and strained dynamics that it was nearly dizzying. The only people she could observe having a conversation without getting vaguely nauseous was Fiona and Maddie. Even at eleven, Maddie still had enough childlike whimsy to engage with Fiona on a level that was nothing but charmed eccentricity.

The conversations between Keaton and Atticus were the most difficult to parse. Every word was loaded with meaning, even when they weren't fighting (or pretending not to fight). Keaton would snipe about something, Atticus would take on a holier-than-thou tone, and it would spiral from there. Frankly, it was exhausting to watch.

Frankie wasn't like any of the rest of them. There was a stillness inside her that made Carsen feel like no matter what hurricane they were in the midst of, she was at the eye of the storm if she was next to her. She was endlessly grateful for it, certain she would've run into the woods to live as a bog witch long ago if not for the anchor of her.

—

That night, she found Frankie standing on the porch, staring vacantly out into the woods, doubtlessly hearing and seeing a hundred tiny things that Carsen's human senses would never be privy to. She moved quietly, trying not to startle her, then wanted to kick herself when Frankie wordlessly reached a hand back to grab hers. Of course, she had heard her. The taller woman drew her up next to her, their bodies pressed up against the railing.

It was the most beautiful night sky she had ever seen. Pitch black, and somehow also a deep blue. Stars scattered across it like freckles, some shining so brightly she thought if she tried she could reach out and touch one. She almost wanted to.

"Watch this," Frankie barely even whispered. Suddenly, she was hollering at the top of her lungs, "Hello!"

Carsen nearly jumped out of her skin and was about to demand what the hell Frankie was thinking, scaring her like that when she heard it.

"Hello! Hello!"

The echo was so soft that she nearly missed it, but the frequency of it carried through the air. She could feel it resonate just under her skin.

She could no longer hold herself back and lifted Frankie's hand from her side to her lips, kissing each rough fingertip, reverent. This moment, this place, this person, they all felt holy to her. Special in a way she hadn't thought existed on

89

this plane.

She made it longer than she had expected before she had her first nightmare there.

Her eyes flew open, a scream ripping her throat. Someone was there, cooing at her soothingly and petting her hair. It took her a moment to calm down enough to see that it was Frankie.

"You're okay. You're fine." She sounded so sure that Carsen wanted to believe her, and she gave a slightly calmer hiccup. When had she started crying? Carsen was such an ugly crier; her mouth would twist so terribly and her nose would stream and her eyes would go puffy, and she was in the back of her mind exceptionally embarrassed that Frankie was here to see it. The front of her mind, however, was too eternally grateful that she was here and that she was keeping her safe from the monsters in her head to care very much.

"It was just a nightmare." The sweet whisper was enough to break the last of the dream's hold on Carsen, and she gave a whooshing final sob before rubbing frantically at her eyes. Frankie pulled her fists away from their rough work, frowning.

"Be gentle." She paused before hesitantly asking, "How do you know which ones are dreams and which are real?"

Carsen remembered a conversation they had had within the first few days of her being there. Frankie had asked her about

90

witch stuff, potions, and spells and divination, and Carsen had told her how she saw the future in her dreams sometimes, how she had since she was a little girl. She had assumed that Frankie would've forgotten it, that she was merely asking to be polite. It was touching that she had deemed it worth remembering.

She cocked her head, considering. "I guess... the real ones sparkle. Well, not sparkle. Just... they feel different. Firmer."

She couldn't quite explain it, honestly. She knew because she knew. It wasn't something to think about, it just *was*. That's how it was about magick most of the time, honestly. Frankie seemed to take this vaguery in stride and simply nodded approvingly, still smoothing Carsen's hair with tender grazing fingers.

"You know, I haven't slept, *really* slept, in weeks[10]. I keep seeing snatches of things, but I can't make it out. It doesn't feel good, though. Something seems wrong."

Frankie hummed sympathetically and moved to rub her back, a slow circle that centered her back into her body.

Suddenly, she realized that it was the middle of the night and that she had, without a doubt, woken her up.

"Oh, Frankie! I'm so sorry. I woke you up, didn't I? Was I loud? Is anyone else awake?" The idea of a whole house of people who weren't quite strangers but seemed like it most of the time hearing her scream made her insides shrivel up

91

in shame. Frankie's lack of comfort confirmed what she had already known. She had yelled and cried and been a baby incredibly loudly in the middle of the night, and every person she was currently trying so hard to impress had heard it and now knew yet another one of her humiliating secrets.

"Nobody is upset with you," Frankie soothed, kissing her forehead. "We were just worried about you."

Carsen felt her face heat up and her stomach drop. *We. Great.*

"I'm sorry," she said again, feeling a little ill.

"Don't be sorry. Are you all good to go?"

Carsen nodded dumbly, and Frankie squeezed her hand once before leaving the room. She could hear low voices in a hushed conversation just outside the door. *Fantastic.*

She sighed and rolled over, preparing herself for the talk tomorrow that she'd encountered everywhere she'd ever lived. *"Maybe you should calm down. Maybe you should see someone. You might be crazy. Have you considered that? Maybe you aren't magick at all. Maybe you're simply mad."* They were all things that she had heard before, but for some reason, the thought of hearing them from anyone here made her heart hurt.

She dawdled as much as possible when the morning fully came, brushing her teeth far longer than necessary and opting for an overly complicated updo for her long brown hair. She was certain that everyone in the house had heard her scream

92

and cry and that if she had been thought of as pathetic before, it was nothing compared to what they would think of her now.

Finally, though, her stomach was grumbling too much to ignore, and she morosely made her way down the stairs.

Keaton and Atticus were sat at the kitchen table, sharing their usual morning cup of blood. Frankie was conspicuously absent from the table. *Probably still asleep since you woke her up in the middle of the night with your whining.* The girls' yelling from outside was only just audible, and she thanked every deity out there that Maddie snored terribly and that, as a result, both her and Fiona slept through anything and everything.

Atticus was the one to see her enter, and he sprang to his feet, sparing a conspicuously meaningful look for the blond still sitting at the table. "Good morning, Carsen! I was thinking I was going to make some French toast. Do you like French toast?"

She had never seen Atticus eat anything for breakfast besides a single boiled egg. They even teased him about it.

"Sure. That sounds nice."

The older man busied himself at the stove, making more noise than strictly necessary. She sat down, a little shy, and suddenly noticed that there was a third cup on the table, this one seemingly not filled with blood.

93

"This is for you," Keaton said gruffly, pushing it across the table to her with an unfathomable expression on his face.

"Oh! Thank you." She took the mug, a little confused, and sat down at the table.

It smelled like lemon balm, lavender, and rosemary. The blend she drank when she was stressed. She took a sip. A drop of honey, no more, no less.

Somehow, Keaton had managed to make her the perfect cup of tea, exactly what she needed, to her exact liking, though she'd never once told him any of her preferences.

Carsen smiled into her mug of tea, her glasses fogging up from the steam.

10

Autumn in F Major, RV. 293: III. Allegro

"Concentrate, Maddie!" Carsen yelled, trying to be heard over the storm.

Maddie turned to look at her and accidentally redirected the rainstorm that was condensed around her head to dump its contents all over Carsen.

She was drenched to the bone instantly and had to focus all her energy on resisting the urge to curse.

"I can't!" Maddie screamed frantically, eyes wild. She could see the girl's chest rising and falling faster and faster, and the winds picking up more with each of her gasps. The sky was darkening by the second, and it was obvious that if she didn't do something soon, their class was going to activate the nearest tornado siren. Carsen took a deep breath and moved towards Maddie, bracing herself against the speeding winds that whipped her hair about. She grabbed the little girl's hand

and leaned in close to be heard over the din.

"We're going to do it together, okay? On the count of the three, you're going to gather all the clouds up and send them away. Picture them blowing apart, each wisp of wind going in a different direction."

"I can't," Maddie croaked, looking like she was being ripped apart from the inside out.

"You can. All this magick in the air is yours - you were strong enough to summon it, and you're strong enough to banish it. Ready?"

The tiniest of nods.

"Okay, let's do it. One."

Maddie squeezed her eyes shut. The wind blew harder.

"Two!" Carsen closed her eyes, too, imagining the storm clouds surrounding them being funneled up into the sky, far away from them.

"Three." It was a quiet whisper from the child, only audible because the air had gone startlingly still all at once.

Carsen opened her eyes. The dark clouds were in retreat, visible in the distance but moving fast.

You did it!" she cheered, turning to look at her charge.

Maddie crumpled to the floor, sobbing hysterically, unable to get a breath. Carsen swan-dived to sit next to her, feeling like gum on the bottom of the world's smelliest shoe.

"It's my fault, I'm sorry. I'm so sorry. I never should have scheduled this so early in the lesson plan. Elemental magick is the most difficult and the most unpredictable. This is my fault, not yours."

Maddie hiccuped, looking bereft. "I can't do anything right."

"No, sweetheart. That's not true at all. You're just learning. Every mistake you ever make is a learning experience! So, what did you learn today?"

The young werewolf said nothing, just continued to cry.

"Do you want to know what I learned?" Carsen asked.

Maddie sniffled, looking at her. Carsen took this as an in, knowing she wouldn't get another one.

"I learned to always bring an umbrella with me to our elemental magick classes!" She wrung her hair out for dramatic effect, the water droplets hitting the ground with a splat. "You would think that I had learned last time, but I'm a goof, so here we are."

Maddie gave a wet laugh, and Carsen felt the tension in the air break. They walked back together, chattering (admittedly mostly her chatter), and by the time she delivered Maddie

97

back to Atticus, there were only a few tear tracks on her face.

"Maddie, go take a warm shower," Atticus said, tone leaving no room for argument. He was growing more and more concerned about her magick and how uncontrolled it seemed to be. Carsen had discussed it many times with him, that it would be like this as she started to develop powers and that it would settle. He remained unconvinced, ever the mother hen father.

Frankie was gently drying Carsen's hair. Carsen relaxed into her touch, relishing the feeling of Frankie's fingertips on her scalp. She saw Atticus raise an eyebrow out of the corner of her eye but ignored it.

"Do you guys usually carve pumpkins for Halloween?" Carsen asked carelessly that evening, as she stood at the kitchen counter preparing sage to dry.

Frankie winced, looking at Fiona, who sat next to her, drawing. The little girl looked as though someone had burned her teddy bear at the stake.

"*Carve* them?" Fiona sounded appalled. Maddie, sitting on the other side of Frankie, popped her head up, looking far too interested.

"Yes?" Carsen said hesitantly, realizing that she had just stepped in it.

"What's carving a pumpkin?" Maddie was now fully engaged.

She was going through a phase right now where anything Fiona even remotely didn't want to do, she suddenly wanted more desperately than she had ever wanted anything in her whole life. The adults were chalking it up to a combination of being cooped up and some sort of hormonal angst, but it was still incredibly inconvenient when she got that look in her eyes. She was about to dig her heels in.

Keaton laughed, disguising it as a cough. He was endlessly entertained by these battles of will, especially when he wasn't the one who would have to deal with it. "Yes, Carsen," he said, the picture of seriousness as he avoided Carsen's glare, "what is 'carving a pumpkin'?"

Carsen looked to Frankie for help but found none there, just a sympathetic face. "Well… During Halloween, sometimes people take out the insides of the pumpkin and put a candle inside. And they cut shapes into the pumpkin so the candle-light shines through, like a decoration." Even having put it as delicately as she could, she could hear how horrifying the activity would be to the young dryad. By the time she had mentioned the insides being taken out there were tears in Fiona's eyes, and by the end, she was full-on crying.

"Carsen, no! That's so mean, we can't do that to them," Fiona insisted. She climbed into Keaton's lap. He combed her hair with his fingers, looking at Carsen with mock indignation. She made a note to herself to give him a good kick to the shins the next time they were alone.

"I want to do it," Maddie said firmly. "Frankie, can't we do it?"

She turned pleadingly to her fellow werewolf, who looked pained.

"Well, I mean... If it means that much to you..."

Fiona started really sobbing then. Loudly.

Crying was where Keaton typically drew the line, and this time was no different. "Alright," he said, clapping his hands as he stood up. "I have an idea. Everyone take a deep breath and calm down, and I'll be right back."

Moments later, he was back, carrying a cardboard box stained with every color under the sun. "I think I have an ethical solution to the murder you're planning on committing," he murmured out the side of his mouth to Carsen, who pouted at him.

"Girls, how about we paint the pumpkins? Fiona, they would be in absolutely no pain, and they'd get to be dressed up, which I'm sure they'll love. Maddie, you can paint *anything* you want."

"*Anything?*" This seemed to have sold Maddie.

"Anything within reason!" Atticus said from the kitchen door, causing them all to jump. Both vampires had a terrible habit of accidentally creeping up on someone and contributing to the conversation without announcing themselves. Carsen had, on more than one occasion, spilled hot tea on herself, jumping from an unknown voice.

Maddie was quiet a moment, seemingly weighing the advantage of unfettered access to Keaton's paints while grieving the fact that it would mean Fiona getting her way. "Alright," she said finally.

Keaton grinned, clearly very pleased with himself. "Let's get started then!"

Carsen took advantage of the chaotic distractions involved in the evening pumpkin painting to slip away to her room and prepare for a little magick. She was finding it harder and harder to keep up her own magickal practice between teaching Maddie and whatever was going on between her, Frankie, and Keaton. Plus, she was always so tired these days.

She was so out of practice that it took a full hour and a half to set everything up, a far cry from her usual twenty-minute routine. Clucking her tongue impatiently with herself, she checked the clock sat on her bedside table. *11:32 PM.* Cutting it close, but she would be fine.

It was pitch black in her room, except for the circle of lit candles she had created in the center of her floor. She had cast a muffling spell on the door to keep her midnight ritual from disturbing anyone. She had perfected it in college after one too many run-ins with an angry roommate.

Carefully stepping over the wall of flame she had created, she settled herself in the very middle of her candle circle, sitting cross-legged. "I call now to my ancestors, to those who came before. It is the night of the crossing, where the veil between those of the now and those of the then is thinnest. I beseech you, as the first-born daughter of Agatha Cromwell, and being of the 23rd generation of Cromwell witches, come forth. I seek thy aid."

Without fanfare, a spirit was suddenly stood in front of her. The first few times she had done a summoning, this had scared the absolute shit out of her, startling her into screaming and losing the connection, but by now, she was an old hand. She appraised the woman in front of her. She had her hair tied back into a tight bun, almost totally obscured by her bonnet and a severe line of a mouth. Most disturbing was the water flowing from her eyes, nose, mouth, and ears. Carsen knew this woman, although she had to admit she was a little disappointed this was the one who had chosen to come get her. She was always so dour.

"Hello, Winnifred. Thank you for coming to see me again," she curtsied. Carsen had had a handful of encounters with this particular ancestor. Winnifred Cromwell had been drowned in a witch trial in rural Massachusetts in 1677 and had been getting the floors wet in Cromwell houses ever since. She showed up more often than any of their other deceased relatives because it was her greatest joy in life (or the afterlife) to pass depressing and obtuse judgment on the plight of the living.

Winnifred's stone face didn't move an inch except to raise her nose in the air and sniff at it. Carsen focused all of her energy on not laughing.

"I smell sin in here, girl. Ungodly things have happened in this room," the old woman intoned, eyes raging with brimstone.

Carsen did not roll her eyes, but it was a close thing. There was something ironic about a witch being so insistent on being holier than thou, but it was Winnifred's specialty, so she tried not to knock it. At least, not while she was on this side of the veil. Besides, what sin could possibly have happened in this room?

Suddenly, the memory of Frankie's rough fingers under the waistband of her underpants, rubbing salve on her hipbone, flooded through her. Carsen wasn't going to pretend that she hadn't had some very unclean thoughts after that had occurred, so she breezed forward, praying that ghosts couldn't read minds. Sometimes it seemed like Winnifred might just be able to, so she whispered a thought-shielding spell under her breath for good measure.

"No unholiness here, ma'am. Just good old-fashioned witchcraft. Speaking of, I was hoping that you could give me guidance on what is to come."

The ghost glowered at her but gave a final indignant sniff and moved closer.

Carsen grimaced but extended her hand out to the body shimmering in the dark. This was her least favorite part of hearing her future, the physical connection with the ghosts needed to make the magick work. She usually preferred to just read her own cards, but the Cromwell line had a bit of extra

103

magickal vigor that she didn't seem to carry, so sometimes it was worth the feeling of having cold water dripped down your spine.

The old woman's veiny fingers reached out and clutched Carsen's young ones, and her eyes slammed shut immediately. Carsen kept hers open, anxiously appraising the spirit, trying to get an idea of what was to come. The woman seemed more upset than usual, eyes fluttering about, face even more tight than it had been before. She suddenly started moaning, ghostly wails that shook the walls. Carsen fought the urge to retract her hand, stomach dropping. This was new.

"The occupants of this house are in grave danger!" The older woman suddenly shrieked, her hand a vice on Carsen's wrist.

"What? What do you mean?" Carsen demanded, trying to get a hold of the transparent sleeve of her dress. Winnifred only moaned louder, reaching a pitch that made Carsen feel as though her eardrums would burst at any moment.

The spirit's eyes popped open, her look wild. "Beware the iron road," she said in a raspy whisper.

An instant later, Carsen's hair was being yanked from her braid by a heavy wind, her candles were blowing out, the papers on her desk were flying everywhere, and Winnifred was gone.

Dour *and* cryptic. Great.

Carsen had to drag herself downstairs the next morning, the ritual having stripped the little energy she usually had right from her marrow. She arrived in the kitchen to an abrupt silence but opted to ignore it in favor of pouring herself a gigantic mug of coffee. When she sat down at the table (more of a flop, really), she could see Keaton and Frankie exchanging glances, but it was the blond boy who finally broke the silence.

"What did you *do* to yourself?" Keaton demanded, looking horrified.

"Wow, thanks." Carsen knew she looked tired - the ceremony had taken place just before midnight, and cleaning up after Winnifred's tirade had taken more than an hour. But surely she couldn't look *that* bad. And if she did, Keaton should have the decency to not comment on it. She looked to Frankie in an appeal for defense but found a similarly aghast expression there.

"...What? What is it?" She was starting to feel a bit nervous with them looking at her like that. Frankie wordlessly stood up and took her hand, gently leading her to the bathroom and shutting the door behind them. Carsen took one look at herself in the mirror and gasped.

Every vein on her thin eyelids looked as though it had been struck by lightning. Blue lines ran up her temples, purple ones under her eyes. Red crept up her neck. The little skin that didn't have bruised veins was gray. Carsen felt tears come to her eyes, and when she blinked them away, she felt the soreness on her eyelids.

105

She was running out of time.

At the edge of the road leading up to the house, the last leaf fell from the oak tree.

II

Winter

11

Tenenbaum

L uckily, the lightning veins didn't stick. Atticus diagnosed them as being a symptom of magickal exhaustion (Carsen loved nothing more than new symptoms). Their resident doctor had informed her that rest and no magick for a few days would set all right again, and it did. It only cost her some of herself and almost all of her concealer to keep it from the girls. It did remind her that she was running low on time, though, and she pushed forward with trying Atticus's litany of experiments regardless of how much they made her hair fall out or her legs wobble.

Winter came suddenly. One night, they went to bed being able to wear just a sweater around the house, and the next, Atticus and Keaton were rounding up wool clothes of every variety to keep warm.

It was quiet that time of year. Fiona had no food to grow, with her garden dead and the ground nearly frozen. Indeed, the dryad seemed a little deadened herself. The rosiness of her cheeks had faded a bit, and her giggle, once a constant presence in the home, was heard less and less frequently. Carsen had been deeply worried that she was getting sick, going so far as to pull Atticus aside, but all was fine. He had explained that during the winters, dryads went into a sort of dormancy, just like their corresponding tree. They slept more, were quieter, felt more emotionally raw, and were generally less like themselves. The whole thing seemed very unpleasant.

It came to a head in mid-November. They were all gathered in the living room, the fireplace roaring cozily. The news was on quietly in the background as they played a board game, Frankie laughing heartily as they caught Maddie doing her best to steal from the banker's money without getting caught.

"Maddie, we can *see* you! Have some shame, for goodness sake," Keaton chided. He was hiding his smile in the corner of his mouth, but the whole room could see it.

Carsen wasn't sure why he bothered trying to hide his obvious affection for the girls. Anybody who heard his voice when Maddie made one of her sniping but strikingly intellectual comments or saw his smiles when Fiona fell asleep on the couch after dinner knew. It was the worst-kept secret in the house, which held an awful lot of poorly kept secrets.

"I don't know what you mean!" Maddie insisted, holding one fist of game money behind her back, trying valiantly not to smile and give herself away any further than she already had.

"Turn it up!" Fiona suddenly cried out, blanching. The

laughter stopped abruptly as they all turned to the TV in the corner.

The TV was a relic from the early 2000s, one of the few pieces of technology in the house beside the stove and Atticus's ancient desktop computer. Maddie's still uncontrolled magick meant that things with wiring were prone to blowing up if she got upset. They also had trouble with gusts of wind knocking down branches when Maddie was forced to go to bed, something that was luckily becoming less frequent as the winter brought earlier sunsets, making her feel like she was staying up later with the grown-ups than she really was.

The old thing was still reliable though, getting the basic channels (including the news, which was what they watched most of the time) and being able to play the DVDs that Atticus had seemingly thousands of. The girls enjoyed having it around, loving to gather the static off of the screen with their hands after it had been turned off for the night, still glowing dimly despite the lack of display.

The screen was filled with terrifying images of forestland burning to the ground. Atticus glanced sideways at Fiona, hesitated, and then begrudgingly crawled over to the base of the TV and increased the volume. He sat back on folded legs to examine the destruction that lay before them in all of 480 pixels.

"Panic today just outside of Sacramento, California as fires rage across the landscape, having already consumed 1,500 acres of forest-"

Fiona made a pitiful groaning sound and flopped onto her back on the floor.

"It's winter, though. I thought fires only happened in the summertime." Maddie was cross-legged on the floor, looking anxiously between her adoptive sister and the screen, which continued to show trees burning to ash.

Carsen wasn't sure how or when Atticus was going to explain climate change to them, but she was very glad that it wasn't her job. She imagined the way Fiona's little face would crumple at the news of what was happening and what was to come and shook her head, willing the image away.

"Why don't we turn off the TV?" Frankie suggested, halfway to her knees to do so.

"No!" Fiona cried out. "We should see. Somebody should have to see." And she burst into tears.

Carsen thought of the agony that Fiona felt at even the prospect of harming a plant and felt her stomach churn at what she must be feeling now.

The veins on Maddie's thin neck stood out from how hard she was clenching her jaw. As much as they fought, the werewitch loved her adoptive sister dearly, and seeing her hurting was clearly agonizing. "Fiona, are you okay?"

The pain of her loss and the weight of her worry was too much for her tiny six-year-old body. Fiona had cried herself into a deep sleep.

Carsen tilted her head back and closed her eyes, wondering how she would bear the ravaged climate to come.

-

It had come to be a habit for them. Every month, Frankie would come home from her night romping through the woods, typically with more than a few gashes across her skin, and Carsen would be up waiting for her with a calming tea, crushed cayenne for pain, and hydrogen peroxide.

At first, Frankie had been hesitant, evidently used to licking her wounds in private all alone, but soon the habit became a comfort for them both.

"It's nice having you around. Obviously not just for this, but... We've never had a healer around before."

"Really?" Carsen was surprised before it clicked in. "Oh. I guess you really don't need one. Your lot isn't as breakable as the people I'm used to."

"I suppose not," Frankie smiled. Suddenly, her warm hand was on Carsen's wrist, holding it gently, as if it could snap if the wind blew too hard. She examined it.

Carsen watched Frankie's burnt umber fingers as they rested gently on her wrist, admired the way they looked against her too-pale skin. "I always forget that you're actually quite fragile. You seem so strong to me."

113

Tears of emotion pricked Carsen's eyes. She had been seen.

"Oh! Oh, what's wrong? Did I say something to upset you?"

Carsen breathed hard. "No. You said something perfect." Suddenly her lips were pressed against the sun that was Frankie.

–

One thing that always bothered Carsen was that it never took too long for Frankie to have the opportunity to return the favor of those moonlit first aid sessions.

"Rough kind of a day[11], huh?" Frankie laid down on the bed next to Carsen, moving slowly so as not to jar her too much. The effort was fruitless but still appreciated.

She'd spent the day laying in the dark, trying not to move and disturb her joints. It hurt enough already. It hurt to breathe. Carsen wanted to be buried under the earth, to grow into something better and more useful than this. Maybe one of Fiona's vegetable plants. Or a fruit tree. She imagined being the cherry that Frankie held in her mouth, closing her eyes to visualize the way that Frankie's tongue carefully removed the pit. Carsen gave the weakest of smiles. She could live with being that cherry.

"What caused it this time?" Frankie inquired, balancing her curly head on her hand as she turned to her side to get a better look at her. The angry part of Carsen wished she wouldn't, wished Frankie would look away until she wasn't this pitiful pathetic thing.

Carsen laughed bitterly. "Me existing caused it. Me waking up this morning caused it."

"That's not fair to you," Frankie said quietly, dark eyes serious and sad, one leg wrapped around Carsen's stomach so she could be a human heating pad for her. Carsen's hips thanked her.

"Life's not fair," Carsen replied, hating how much she sounded like her mother.

"You're a bitter kind,[12]" Frankie teased, gazing at Carsen like she moved the earth and sky. She leaned forward and kissed her. "Sour. I like that."

Carsen grinned back, only a little half-heartedly.

That night, as they lay in bed next to each other, catching their breath, Carsen wondered how long something this good could last.

12

Motion Sickness

C arsen sat in the living room, curled in the overstuffed chair with her prized copy of *Pride and Prejudice* in her lap when a drop of water landed on the page.

She blinked, horrified, as she watched the paper immediately begin to sag from the dampness. She quickly, deftly, wiped the water from the page, but another drop came, and another. She lifted a hand to her face. She was crying.

"Huh," she said quietly, trying to identify what the feeling was that was causing the ache in her throat.

"What's wrong?" Frankie asked, lowering herself to squat in front of the chair and look up at her.

"It's nothing, just allergies."

"It's wintertime," Frankie noted.

Carsen broke down. "I miss my mom. Like a little kid[13], I miss her. Like the way you felt being dropped off at kindergarten for the first time."

Frankie sighed and plopped down next to her, banging her hip against hers to get Carsen to scooch over. "I know. I've been watching you for the last couple of days. Is there something specific that's causing it, or is it just the time passing?"

"It's the wintertime, I think. This is my favorite time of year. We always go to Boston and look at the Christmas decorations."

"You and your mom?" Frankie pressed.

"Yeah. Me and my mom."

"You could write to her, you know. We have stamps and envelopes here."

Carsen chewed on her lip. "I don't think I can. Not yet." Writing would mean apologizing. She had never gotten a return letter from the one she had sent when she first arrived, and Carsen knew what that meant. Her mother would not respond until she had gotten an apology.

She thought of their fight and the things she had said and winced. No, not yet. She would need to lick her wounds for a little longer.

They sat in the living room that night, all six of them, the fire crackling, Keaton teaching Maddie how to play euchre. It was a Midwest classic card game, befitting their Ohio homestead.

Atticus looked up at Carsen, who sat in the same seat as she had earlier that day during her impromptu cry sesh, and smiled.

"Carsen, why don't you tell us about your home?"

Carsen wanted to smack herself in the face. The door to the living room had been wide open. Anyone could have heard her and Frankie's conversation, and clearly, someone had.

Frankie looked mortally offended by Atticus's suggestion. "I don't think-"

"It's fine." Carsen interrupted. Why not? She had felt lighter after telling Frankie about the Christmas lights, after all. Maybe it would help. "So I'm from Salem, Massachusetts. My family is a very old clan of witches, dating back to the witch trials, and Cromwells have lived in the same house for two hundred years."

"Witch trials?" Maddie asked, sounding deeply concerned.

Carsen nearly cursed aloud. Whoops. Probably not the best topic for a young, impressionable witch.

"I'll tell you about them later," Keaton reassured her, eyes on Carsen.

"Yes, and I can help you do that," Carsen said, throwing Keaton an appreciative look. "So. The house is two hundred-some years old, and it's full of magick. Everybody who lives there has their name written into the wood of the house somewhere. It's wherever they spend the most time, usually. We think it's the house absorbing our energies and manifesting its acceptance of the occupant. It's been that way for generations. Anybody who occupies the family home has their name in a place that's theirs."

"Where's your name written?" Keaton asked, voice soft.

Carsen smiled at the memory. "There's a bookshelf in the living room. My name is all over it. Beautiful cursive."

"Is your name still there?" Frankie asked.

"Of course. It'll stay there till the house knows I'll never live there again."

"So you'll go back?" Frankie asked dismally.

"Yes, after Maddie is done learning everything I can possibly teach her," Carsen answered, not making eye contact with Frankie. She hadn't actually thought about it until that very moment. Would her name still be in the house after that fight with her mother? After her decision to leave, even for a while, being so violent? Surely it would, wouldn't it?

Carsen couldn't sleep that night, thinking about amber and blue eyes and how she might never see them again.

"Are we ready for our field trip?" Frankie asked, pulling a beanie over her dark hair.

The girls had been clamoring for weeks to go to the lake and see it frozen over. Carsen had to admit that even she was a little excited despite the bitter cold that they would be willingly subjecting themselves to. It only happened a few times every decade, and Atticus had heard from the butcher that a few mornings ago, it was daggers of ice all the way across.

It wasn't terribly far, only about a twenty-minute walk from the house. Atticus and Fiona stayed, keeping the fire going and the hot chocolate warm, and the rest of them tromped out into the elements. By the time they'd traveled a half mile, Carsen was starting to get grumpy, but they suddenly came out of the woods and up onto the lake, and she saw it was all worth it.

It was awe-inspiring, with the whole lake entirely frozen over. Where the water came to land, it had frozen into little waves, creating thousands of daggers of ice. Several townspeople were out doing the same thing they were, but they ignored them in favor of each other's company.

"Are you ready for a tale?" Keaton asked in a silly voice, wiggling his wool-covered fingers. Carsen pointed a finger, disguised by her mittens, and a wind whisked across the lake, an outline of a person dancing, and Maddie oohed and ahhed appreciatively.

120

"Now, the story goes that a long time ago, a family from Scotland came to America. They had a son. I think he was about your age, Maddie. This boy was terribly sad to be leaving his home, especially because he would have to leave his best friend." Keaton had a lovely voice, low and melodic, and the girls liked nothing better than his storytelling. Carsen would never admit it, but she often was just as transfixed as the girls were.

"The family had lived next to a river," he continued, "and the boy went there every day to visit what he thought was a horse. They would take turns running through the water, splashing, and playing. The horse would let him ride on its back, and they would run so fast that the boy felt like he was flying."

Carsen whisked up an apparition of a horse from the ice shards and let it run in front of them across the lake.

"It wasn't a horse, of course, but a kelpie," Keaton continued. "A ghost of sorts. Now, kelpies usually hate humans, but this one was different. He cared for the boy, and the boy cared for him. When the boy left with his family, he could hear the horse neighing for him to come back. They made it to America and found a home on the frontier. The boy had enjoyed the adventure and took to his new home, but he still missed Scotland and his horse. One day, not long after they arrived, he went to a nearby stream and sat near the water, thinking about his friend back home. Suddenly, he heard the clopping of hooves. He looked up, and his friend stood in front of him, water rushing over its legs. Somehow the kelpie spirit had gotten stuck in the boy's soul, and so he had traveled

121

with him all the way across the ocean."

Maddie was absolutely still, eyes round and as big as dinner plates. "Can that really happen?" She looked to Carsen and Frankie to confirm that Keaton wasn't pulling her leg, and Carsen nodded solemnly.

"Even wilder things than that happen every day. That's why we always tell you and Fiona not to go into the woods alone. Our world may be magickal, but it's also incredibly dangerous. There are things out there that don't have your best interests at heart," Frankie said, flush high on her cheeks.

Carsen squeezed Frankie's hand. She could've sworn she heard hoofbeats.

13

It's Alright

The first snow came early that year, and December was barely a week old by the time they were all bundled up outside among the snowflakes. The flakes came down fast, piling up among the strands of grass in a way that left just the tips of each blade showing.

Fiona and Maddie, wrapped up to their eyes in identical tiny parkas and knitwear, were busily making a snowman. There really wasn't enough snow on the ground to make much of anything, but Carsen had done an enchantment before they went out, and the girls always seemed to have just enough for the next body part they were making. They had taken some stale jelly beans from the back of the pantry and were making buttons and eyes out of them. One of Fiona's pickled zucchinis from the summer was serving as a nose. It looked like the sort of meal you made when you were about two days past when you should've gotten groceries, and Maddie and Fiona were enamored by their beautiful work.

The adults were engaged in a supernatural snowball fight. Atticus and Keaton, both bulky with layers of sweaters, had excellent aim. Frankie couldn't hold on to the snowball for any length of time, or it would melt in her overly warm hands, but that was alright because she moved with lightning speed, positively pelting the vampires without mercy. The two bloodless boys looked a little miserable, and Carsen knew that as cold as she was, they were at least ten degrees colder. Keaton, in particular, looked as though he was on the verge of frostbite. His gloves were soaking wet, and she could see his thin fingers shaking. It was a little pitiful (though, of course, she would never say such a thing to his face), and she winced as he got nailed by a particularly large snowball courtesy of Frankie, who seemed to have no such sympathies. The werewolf absolutely cackled with glee, and to Carsen's shock, Keaton laughed too.

She had been noticing more and more the way that Keaton was around Frankie. Frankie was friendly and loving with everyone, so her kisses pressed to his blond curls in the morning didn't mean much of anything. But Keaton had a habit of being hard, not affectionate with anyone if he could help it. That's why it was always so surprising to see him leaving his hand on Frankie's a bit longer when they passed a serving bowl at dinner or the way he saved a special smile just for her in the mornings. He was always very polite with all the girls, that bit of the traditional Southern gentleman who lingered in him, but with Frankie, it was as if she was a princess. She never opened a door if he could help it, or pulled out her own chair. It made Carsen feel the tiniest ugly twist in her stomach, and she was furious with herself about it. She wasn't an envious person, but when she saw the easy way the two smiled at each other, she went green.

She wasn't sure what she was jealous of or whom, and it made her a little nervous. Carsen worked very hard to keep an iron hand on her emotions, tracing each one to its source and handling them accordingly. She and Frankie weren't anything solid, not yet, just two people who kissed and sometimes shared a bed. She had no right to be mad if Frankie beamed when Keaton chastely kissed her cheek before he left a room.

And, if she was honest, she was in no small amount jealous *over* Frankie rather than of her. She had poured every ounce of charm in her admittedly small body into trying to get Keaton to like her, and she had still barely broken the icy exterior. He had seemed to have gotten over actively wanting her to leave, but still, there was always a distance in the way that he interacted with her that made her feel a bit lonely.

"Carsen! What kind of battle partner are you? Get over here!" Frankie called cheerfully, jarring her out of her reverie.

Carsen herself was doing her best to stay out of the fray, standing on the outskirts of the battleground and enchanting snowballs to hover and fling themselves at her opponents. Every so often, she would heft a particularly large one, and when it dropped onto someone's head, she would get the satisfaction of a violent curse. She had noticed that Atticus and Keaton somehow always seemed to miss her, while Frankie got a faceful of snow every other minute. She wanted to be a bit offended but instead found herself touched by it.

"Sorry!" She limped her way closer to them, cursing the way that the cold was settling in her joints, making them even more stiff and sore.

"I'm freezing," Keaton said suddenly. They all looked at him. He did look like an icicle, snow frozen to his eyelashes and his nose streaming. Still, it wasn't like him to complain.

"I am as well. I made some hot chocolate earlier if we'd like to come to a truce for now." Atticus somehow looked dignified, even puffed up with his quilted coat that was zipped straight up to his chin. "Besides, if the girls put one more piece of candy on that snowman, I think he'll fall over."

They looked over to see the snowman absolutely covered in brightly colored food, mostly pieces of candy. The girls had gone back into the pantry without them realizing it, and a candy suit and tie had taken shape. A beanie that Carsen recognized as belonging to Atticus was on its head. It was overkill but lovely overkill, and Carsen made a mental note to take a picture of it later.

"Time to go in, girls!" Frankie called. The two little ones turned from their creation and started running towards the house, the adults following close behind them.

Their painted pumpkins sat on the front porch underneath a snow blanket that kept them from rotting. Fiona's green smiley face beamed out at them from beneath the flurries, and Carsen smiled back at it happily.

–

It was getting close to midnight, and Keaton and Carsen were the only ones left in the living room. It was a fairly small space that they spent limited time in, and yet it still somehow managed to be in a constant state of disarray.

Pictures covered the wall, a sort of memorial to all the lives the immortals among them had lived (with plenty of pictures of the girls on every possible holiday, even Arbor Day), and sometimes, when Carsen couldn't sleep, she'd come in and examine them. She found something new every time. A picture of Atticus in Edinburgh, at the top of Arthur's Seat. An artistic shot of Frankie as a wolf and another of her paw prints trailing through the snow. Keaton, in black and white, hoisting a protest sign railing against poor working conditions, face stern. When you sat with them every day and saw them with oatmeal on their shirts and sleepy-eyed from having just woken up, it was easy to forget that Atticus and Keaton had been alive far longer than they looked.

They sat in companionable silence, safe in the knowledge that everyone else in the house was either asleep or on their way there. Both sat in overstuffed armchairs that had seen better days. They each clutched books: nonfiction for Keaton and a cozy mystery for Carsen. She hadn't even noticed that she had started picking at her skin, a nervous habit she'd had since she was a teenager, until Keaton said something.

"Hey... Carsen, stop that." His hands went for hers, but not in time. She'd ripped the skin. A drop of blood fell from the place on her forehead she'd been furiously picking at. Keaton inhaled sharply. Visions of Keaton lunging across the armchair and sinking his fangs into her forehead made Carsen go a bit weak.

"Sorry, sorry, oh my God, I'm so sorry." She shot up from the chair, eyes wide, a mix of apologetic and frightened.

Keaton merely looked at her. "Whatever are you sorry for?" he said simply, leaning over to get a handkerchief out of his pocket. He handed it to her and returned to his reading, acting as though he was not a bloodthirsty creature who took blood in a travel mug with him everywhere.

She must've looked really ill because Keaton glanced up and immediately put his book down and examined her closely, eyes narrowed. "Are you quite alright?"

Even as she desperately tried to staunch the bleeding, she couldn't help but roll her eyes. Every time she almost forgot that he wasn't from now, he reminded her, whether in a strange turn of phrase or an endearing old-fashioned habit like this one.

"I figured the blood would... upset you. I don't know. Doesn't it?"

He wheezed a laugh, sounding vaguely feral. The noise made Carsen regret asking.

"Not particularly. I haven't had human blood directly from the source in some time." He seemed to have decided that she was regaining color at a rate he was comfortable with and pulled his book back up to reading position. His eyes didn't return to the pages, though, staying locked on her.

"Oh. I'm sorry, I didn't mean to imply-" Carsen stammered. Who would've thought that discussing someone's dietary habits could be such a minefield?

"It's perfectly fine and a reasonable and courteous question for you to have asked." It was a little stilted, but he didn't seem offended, so Carsen decided to be brave.

"Why did you stop? Drinking 'directly from the source'?"

Keaton's book dropped into his lap, and she suddenly realized how unpardonably rude it was for her to have asked such a thing.

"Oh God, I'm so sorry, you don't have to answer-"

"Carsen." His voice was even, and he had lost the ruffled look on his face, now appearing merely amused.

"I stopped drinking from humans directly about... 20-some years after I became a vampire. Not long, in the scheme of things, for someone who lives forever. Nothing particular happened to cause it. It's hardly like they have documentaries about inhumane human farming. Though they might now... The Internet is such a wonderful thing." This was such an odd thing to hear come out of his mouth that she nearly giggled, but she kept her composure.

129

"I just hated having to do it. I always had, even from the very first time. I didn't see another way, though. I would try and go without it, go days, and then I would nearly collapse from the strain and have to give in and feel even worse for having failed so miserably in the process. It was only when I met Atticus at the World Fair in 1893 that I learned that there might have been another way."

This was the most Keaton had ever said at one time to Carsen, and she was shocked that he was admitting these things so openly. "How did you know he was a vampire too?"

Keaton smiled. "He was the only one in the crowd without a heartbeat."

This startled her a bit. "You don't have a heartbeat?"

As soon as she finished asking it, she knew how stupid she sounded, and she went red with embarrassment at how obviously unknowledgeable she was. Keaton didn't comment, though, merely held out his hand to her, palm up. She looked at it, brows furrowed.

"You can feel for a pulse if you want."

Taking the rare opportunity, she reached out and touched his wrist, looking at where the veins would've been, should've been pumping blood. There was indeed no pulse there.

"It was silly to ask. It's just that…you seem so human."

Keaton's face closed yet again, and she cursed her inability to keep her ridiculous mouth shut.

"No matter what I look like, I'm certainly no human. I'm a monster."

"You're not a monster[14]," she whispered.

He sighed, looking over at her with an expression she couldn't read. "I know what I am. You need to know it, too."

They sat quietly for a while again, Carsen berating herself for messing up what had been such a lovely conversation. As they watched the fire, feeling its warmth wash over them and listening to its crackle, she could feel sleep passing over her. She swallowed a yawn, but the non-human next to her noticed.

"You should go to bed." His voice was cordial and stern at the same time, a combination he seemed to have mastered. It seemed like a dismissal, so she took it as one.

"Alright. Good night." She stood up and made it halfway to the door before she heard his voice again.

"Carsen?"

"Yes?" she answered, turning around.

He just looked at her bleakly. "Sleep well."

A few days later, she found herself outside Keaton's room, hand shaking as she knocked on the door. She hadn't been in Keaton's room since he'd been sick in the fall. A few times a week, she'd be in her room next to his and hear him playing the cello, and once in a very long while, when she was up late, she would hear him shifting in his sleep, but this once-removed listening was as close as she got.

"Yes?" He opened the door, holding a paperback book open with one hand. "Carsen, is everything okay?"

"Oh, yeah! Yeah. I just... I have something for you."

He raised his eyebrows suspiciously. "...You do?"

"I do, yes." She brought a wrapped package out from behind her back. "It's not much."

He furrowed his brow, smiling a bit. "May I?" He reached out, and their fingers brushed. The static of the cold weather gave them a spark, and Carsen flinched. Keaton didn't comment; he just took the package and ripped the paper.

"It's like Christmas came early," he commented, looking at her, not the candy cane wrapping paper she had chosen.

"Oh!" He had gotten it open and was holding the gift in his hands like it was gold and not the knit mittens she had made over the last two days.

"Carsen, you shouldn't have. They must've taken ages."

132

They were some of her better work, a Fair Isle argyle pattern and a thick ribbing for around his wrists. She smiled, allowing herself a bit of self-satisfaction.

"Put them on." It came out bossier than she had expected, and she felt like apologizing for it, but Keaton seemed unbothered. He slipped the knits on, still looking astonished. When his hands were inside of them, he made another surprised sound.

"Oh! They're so warm."

"I put a little charm on them. To keep your hands from freezing. You seemed so miserable the other day when we were outside. I thought they might help. I don't know if the magick will hold forever. I might have to redo the spell every once in a while, and I dropped a few stitches-"

"They're perfect. I love them. Thank you, Carsen. This was very kind of you." Keaton looked a bit thunderstruck, staring at his hands.

She smiled. "No problem. I'll leave you alone now." She turned to go but felt a mittened hand wrap around her wrist.

"Do... Would you like to borrow a book? I have some I think you might like, and I noticed that you had almost finished with the one you were reading last night."

Carsen felt hope spring up in her chest and stepped through the bedroom door.

14

Keep Yourself Warm

"This week, we're going to work on the different forms of divination," Carsen said cheerfully. "I think we'll start with scrying for today, and then tomorrow, we'll bust out the tea leaves. And if you feel good about those, we can use my tarot cards."

They were having class outside even though it was bitterly cold. Carsen, although she knew it was a bit of a hard ass thing to do, always insisted on it. Her mother had always told her that magick works best when you're in nature, with your feet on a dirt floor and your mind under an open sky. She held to that like the only sort of gospel a witch can have, and so they were outside, breaths puffing visibly into the air and wearing gigantic jackets and unwieldy mittens. Frankie had forced Carsen to wear *two* scarves, and she felt as though she was wearing some sort of neck cast. She was warm though so Frankie (as per usual) had been right.

"What's scrying?" Maddie asked, blowing on her hands and

leaning from foot to foot to keep warm. Her cheeks were bright red, but Carsen knew that she wasn't as cold as she was making herself out to be.

Frankie had been checking her average temperature each month since she'd turned eleven as a barometer for how close she was to the change. There'd been a steady increase the last two months, and now she was hanging out at a steady 101 degrees. It was hardly Frankie's 110, but it was an indicator that things were on their way.

"I'm so glad you asked." Carsen was unusually chipper, something she knew was grating for the angsty pre-teen, but she couldn't help it. Divination was her favorite magick practice, and she had a feeling that Maddie would take to it even better than she had to sigil work. "Plop on down."

She lowered herself to the icy ground to sit cross-legged in front of the velvet cover obscuring a small sphere. She whipped it off with a flourish to reveal a crystal ball balanced on a three-pronged moon design.

"I got my fancy crystal ball out just for you." It had been incredibly heavy in her suitcase on the way here, but the way that Maddie now looked impressed against her will made it worth it.

"So here's how this works. Sit, sit." She patted the ground next to her, and begrudgingly, Maddie sat.

"We start by taking a deep breath and centering all of our

energy into our mind's eye. Think of nothing else but what you desire. And what do we desire?"

"To go back inside," Maddie said under her breath.

"That's right. We want to see what the future holds for us. Now, as you get better at it you'll be able to see the futures of people more peripheral to you, but it's easiest to see your own or people close to you, so, for now let's start with that."

Maddie, despite her best intentions, was starting to look the teeniest bit excited.

"So. Deep breath. Look at the ball and ask it what is to come."

"What is to come?" Maddie's voice came out strong, and Carsen smiled.

"Very good. We can also say it in our head, but I think saying it out loud might trigger a stronger reaction, especially when you're first starting out. Now, what do you see?"

Maddie concentrated for a moment, brow furrowed and eyes squinted, staring at the ball like her life depended on it. "I see...I see snow! A snowflake falling."

Fifteen seconds after the words left her mouth, a single snowflake floated to the earth, landing on the crystal ball and melting to oblivion.

Carsen cheered and hugged Maddie, who was beaming

proudly, all attempts at nonchalance gone.

"That was amazing, Maddie! You're going to be an amazing seer; I just know it. Okay, that was quite enough work for one day. I think if we go inside and ask nicely, Frankie will make us some hot chocolate."

Maddie shot to her feet and sprinted inside, clearly dying to share her news. Carsen moved a little slower, leaving the crystal ball for Frankie or Keaton to carry inside (probably Frankie - the thing was heavier than it looked). As she crossed the threshold, she bit back a grin. Frankie stood there waiting, a cup of hot chocolate outstretched.

Everything was perfect.

–

Carsen woke up to a tiny cherub poking her in the side, anxiously muttering.

"What? What?" She startled awake and then shook herself. Fiona was stood by her bedside, looking beseechingly at her.

"Oh! Fiona, what's wrong? Are you okay?"

"Maddie is gone."

"She's gone? Gone where?" Carsen rolled out of bed with a speed that she hadn't achieved in years.

"She said she had to leave. She said it wasn't safe, and she wouldn't listen to me."

"When was this?" Carsen asked, suddenly very awake.

"I don't know. Not very long."

Carsen worked very hard not to curse. "Okay. Everything is going to be fine. Go back to sleep, okay? I'll take care of it, I promise." She walked Fiona to her room, watched the door close, then pinwheeled wildly and found herself running down the hallway, halfway out of her body. She pounded on Frances' and Keaton's doors as she passed, frantically yanking on a coat and searching for her boots. Keaton was in the hallway instantly, his mad mop of blond curls even more mussed than usual.

"What? What's wrong?" His voice was groggy, and if the circumstances weren't so dire she would've felt bad for waking him. He had such a hard time sleeping as it was, without search parties gathering in the middle of the night.

By the time Carsen had hopped back down the corridor, one boot halfway on, Frances had emerged as well, looking sleepy, her hair knotted.

"Carsen?" she asked, her voice soft with sleep.

"Maddie ran away. Fiona said she left a few minutes ago."

"Now?" Keaton's eyes widened. Frances had returned to her room and could be heard tearing through her closet.

"Why would she do that? What happened?" Frances reemerged, a hat yanked over her tangled braids and a huge coat on. In her hand was another knit cap, which she threw to Keaton. He caught it without a word or a glance, still staring terrified at Carsen.

"She had a dream. Or a vision, I'm not sure. She thinks there's some sort of danger. We were working on scrying today. Maybe it stirred something up. I don't know. We have to *go!*" Carsen urged.

"I'll wake Atticus." Frances flew past them, running to the room at the end of the hall.

"We should bring a coat for her, for when we find her," Keaton mumbled, looking around as though one would appear within arms reach.

"I'll get it. You get a coat," Carsen said. "Or maybe don't come, I don't know if you'll do well in these temperatures."

"I'll get a coat," he said acidly, turning back into his room with his shoulders set.

Atticus swept down the hallway, looking effortlessly graceful in comparison to Frances's half-awake stumbling, a step behind him.

"Are you three going to go after her?" He was all business, like a military commander ordering troops into battle. In the back of her mind, Carsen wondered if he ever had been. She

139

stowed the thought away for later, shoving away thoughts of Atticus in 1700s military garb.

"I don't think Keaton and Carsen should come," Frances said, wincing as the two in question began to loudly protest. "Especially Keaton. It's below freezing out there, and I can handle it, and so can Maddie for now, but it could get bad fast."

"We're coming." Carsen put as much sternness in her tone as she could muster and felt gratified to see Keaton nodding vigorously at her, even as he zipped up a second sweater, holding a puffy jacket in his arms.

"Alright. I'll stay here with Fiona. Maybe she'll come back on her own. Go quickly." Atticus looked like he was carved from stone, his sharp cheekbones looking fiercer than ever in the half-light. They were out the door in an instant, tumbling over one another in their haste.

The snow was a sheet, swirling fiercely around them like it was the atmosphere itself coming to life. It battered Carsen's face, stinging with cold.

"We should split up. We'll find her faster," Frances said, looking frantic. Her legs were moving twice as fast as Carsen's, and she had to break into a light jog to keep up with her.

"Yeah, and we'll also get separated, and one of us will freeze to death out here," Keaton said sharply. He was already looking a bit blue around his nose and lips, and Carsen shuddered to think what state he'd be in by the time they found Maddie.

"Think. Where would she go?"

"The fort?"

"Worth a try." They forged forward. The single snowflake from earlier had turned into a flurry of them, and they caught everywhere. Their hair, their jackets, their skin. On Frankie, they merely melted right off, but Carsen and Keaton both looked like they had a terrible case of dandruff right down to their eyelashes.

They moved more quickly than Carsen found strictly comfortable, but she didn't complain. Somehow, on some level, she couldn't help but feel that this was her fault. She was the one who had encouraged Maddie to look into her future. It hadn't even occurred to her that that future might not be a warm and welcoming one.

"Can you see in the dark[15]?" Carsen asked, realizing how sure-footed the other two were compared to her bumbling.

The way that they both said yes, as though it was nothing made her feel even more inadequate than before.

It felt like they had been out there for years, but in reality, it couldn't have been more than twenty minutes of the trio yelling for Maddie and checking behind each tree before they saw a small thin figure, dark hair stark against the snow.

"Maddie!" Frankie snatched her up in her arms like a terrified mother seizing a child after a few moments of losing them in the supermarket. She ran her hands all over her body, frantically asking, "Are you hurt?" Even after Maddie said several times that she was fine, Frankie was still in a panic, and it took Keaton's gentle touch on her back to bring her out of it.

"I'm fine, Frankie," Maddie said, looking a little shell-shocked. Carsen wasn't sure if it was the lateness of the hour, the adrenaline of the adventure, or the way that three grownups' full attention was focused on her, but there was something in Maddie's eyes that screamed not all there.

"What were you thinking, running away like that? Anything could have happened, anything could have gotten you." Frankie was nearing hysterics once again, but a sideways glance from Keaton brought her back down.

"We can figure that out later," Keaton gritted out, teeth chattering so hard it was a miracle he didn't bite his tongue off. "It's freezing, let's go home." He was shaking so hard that his whole body looked like it was experiencing a never-ending earthquake. Could vampires freeze to death? If he was out here much longer, they might be the first ones to find out.

Carsen appraised Keaton's miserable face before glancing at Frankie, hoping she would have some sort of solution now that she was thinking clearly with Maddie back within reach. As always, Frankie came through.

142

"There's a cave nearby that I go to during the full moon. It's not super roomy, but it is warm, and we could wait out the storm there."

Keaton looked like he might argue, but Carsen agreed so vehemently that he had no choice but to follow Frankie deeper into the woods.

The cave was indeed not roomy, with barely enough room for them all to squeeze in together and be out of the mouth of the cave where the storm was still raging, wind beating against the rock face. Carsen quickly made a fire just inside the cave, snapping her fingers to start the blaze. It was the sort of showy, energy-draining magick she tried to avoid at all costs, but this was an emergency.

They all settled in, Keaton so close to the fire that Carsen had to stop herself from pulling him away. They sat in an awkward silence for a while, just watching the snowflakes fall furiously.

"Why did you run, Maddie?" Keaton was the one to ask it, which was a surprise to both of the women, but they kept quiet, waiting for Maddie's answer.

"I saw it," she whispered, sounding quite desolate. "I saw me change. And it was awful. Frankie, it hurt so much! Why didn't you tell me it would hurt? I felt everything, and it felt like I was being shredded inside out. Why didn't you tell me it's going to feel like that?" Her tenses were everywhere, clearly still half in her vision and not fully able to separate the future from the present.

Frankie pursed her lips for a moment before taking a deep breath. "It does hurt, yes. Especially that first time. You'll feel like you were ripped apart afterward, probably for a few days. I hurt for a week after my first time. You'll be terribly sore. Like you ran two marathons with no training. It'll be like your skin is too thin to hold everything in."

It was utterly quiet besides the crackling of the fire and Frankie's voice. She never talked about this, never talked about the change, and even when she did it was only in the vaguest of terms. The sincerity was a little frightening.

"But when you're a wolf," Frankie continued, "you don't feel any of that. You're a part of nature, different from the way that Carsen has been teaching you to be. You understand the birds, the deer. You can hear the trees talking to each other. You feel the worms under your feet when you run." She turned to face Maddie fully. The girl was enraptured, eyes wide, halfway between fear and appreciation.

"You won't be human, and you won't be animal. You'll be an in-between thing. And it'll be scary and lovely, and you'll never be able to quite work out which feeling is strongest. But listen to me, okay? We are lucky. To have this gift. It hurts, and it can be inconvenient, but we get to walk in two worlds in a way that not even these two do." She jerked a thumb at Carsen and Keaton.

"And you, you're even luckier than the rest of us. You have

magick, Maddie. I can't even dream of what your change will be like. I can only imagine it'll feel like being tapped into an electric grid powerful enough to run the whole world. You will be so strong and so beautiful. And yes, it will hurt. But life hurts anyway. So wouldn't you rather get to feel all that?"

It was verbose even for Frankie's typical soliloquies, and after she finished speaking, everyone was stunned into silence. Time passed in a way that didn't feel quite real, and it passed quickly.

Finally, Keaton gently said, "Maddie?"

The little werewolf was dead asleep, head resting crookedly against the cave wall in a way that had to be incredibly uncomfortable. Frankie gave an amused little huff, and gently readjusted the girl so that she was laying with her head on her lap.

"I hope she heard at least some of that. It was some of my best work."

Carsen and Keaton kept quiet, still a bit unsure what to say. In the silence, they wormed their way to be tighter against Frankie, Keaton lifting Maddie easily so that her body was on top of him, letting her remain pillowed on Frankie's thigh. Frankie was their own space heater they barely needed the fire, but they kept it for the light that it provided, looking at each other's faces and waiting for the first one to speak and break the spell.

145

"You were really good with her, Frankie." Keaton's voice was quiet and warm, more affectionate than Carsen had ever heard him. Frances looked a strange mix of pleased and sad.

"Well, I know what it's like. To be afraid like that." Her voice was small and sad, in a way that Frankie never was, and Carsen's heart was tugged into her stomach.

Almost at the same time, Keaton and Carsen's hands came to meet the clasped set on Frances's lap. In silent agreement, they each took one.

"I didn't know it was bothering her so much. I thought I was helping by not talking about it. She never wanted to, so I followed her lead. Maybe I was just being a wimp though. Not wanting to talk about the hard things." Frankie's russet face held the light from the fire in a way that made her look angelic. She turned her head to look at Keaton.

"Was I wrong?"

"You did what you thought was best. And that's all any of us can do." His voice was firm and final, and they could feel Frankie relax under its sincerity.

Carsen was half-asleep now and allowed her eyes to fully close, willing herself the rest of the way.

–

They made their way back to the house by six that morning, a bedraggled bunch, all exhausted and frozen. Atticus was

146

waiting, not impatiently or worriedly, but expectantly.

"Oh no! We should've done something to let Atticus know everything was okay. He must have been worried sick," Carsen fretted.

"It's fine. I let him know," Keaton said shortly. He had warmed up in the cave but immediately lost all the progress the moment they had left it, and the chill made him grouchier than normal.

She side-eyed him. "You 'let him know'? How? When?"

Frankie laughed, a guffaw really, and the release made Carsen smile even though she had no idea what she was laughing about.

"Vampires can talk to each other. In their heads, I mean. You've really been too quiet about your gifts. Why didn't you tell her?" She directed this question at Keaton, jabbing him in the ribs with an elbow. He yelped inelegantly in answer and gingerly rubbed at his ribs. It was lucky he didn't have any blood running through his veins, or he would certainly have bruised.

"Are there *no* secrets in this house? I'd like to keep at least some mystery."

Maddie ran straight into Atticus's arms, and his slightly pinched expression evaporated on contact.

147

"Go inside and see your sister, dear. She's been very worried about you," he said sternly.

Head down in penance, Maddie made her way to the porch, looking back once before shoving the door open and entering. All four adults watched, breathing a sigh of relief as she crossed the threshold. *Crisis averted. Somewhat.*

"Is everyone else alright?" This seemed mostly directed at Keaton, who was luckily only slightly blue but still looking a bit too much like Jack Frost for anyone's liking.

"Fine. We're all fine." Frankie supplied, rubbing Keaton's arm roughly to warm him.

"Nothing some soup and talking won't fix. We do have to do something about Maddie, though. I think this is going to get worse before it gets better."

-

After all the excitement of the night, the day felt almost dull. Though maybe that was the lack of sleep, Frankie nearly dropped off into her mashed potatoes during dinner. They sent the girls to bed early, then sat at the table, quietly examining the pockmarks of the wood, pretending they weren't all thinking the same thing.

Finally, Keaton cleared his throat. "I think someone should stay outside her bedroom tonight. Just in case. A precautionary measure." His nerves made him verbose, and he would've kept listing synonyms that tried to convince them how not worried he was if they hadn't cut him off.

"I agree," Frankie said.

Carsen nodded. "I'll sleep out there, it was my fault I got her all worked up, and she ran away." She hadn't expected such an intense response.

"Absolutely not-"

"Of course, it's going to be me-"

Atticus raised his hand, and this particular brand of magick of his worked even on grown adults.

"I have a compromise," he said gently.

And that's how they all ended up curled up in front of the girls' door, sound asleep, tangled together. There was something profoundly lonely about hearing Keaton and Frankie breathe in tandem, so close to her and yet a million miles away. Carsen rolled over with a sigh to focus on watching the door.

She wouldn't let Maddie be in harm's way again.

-

She woke up to Fiona falling into their person pile, startling all three of them awake at once. She blinked at them owlishly. "Why are you guys here?"

"Special grownup sleepover," Frankie supplied, trying to look casual with her long legs sprawled out everywhere and hair in Keaton's mouth.

"Hm." Fiona looked a thousand years old just then, giving them a knowing look not at all fitting someone still several months short of her seventh birthday.

They traipsed to the kitchen, where Frankie, yawning nearly nonstop, put on the kettle.

Keaton opened the fridge, then shut it, brow furrowed. "What day is today?"

"Thursday," Carsen murmured as she stood at the sink watching the world outside.

"We're out of blood. Earlier than usual. I wonder if Jim dropped off less accidentally last week."

"He had fewer meat orders last week, for some reason. Apparently, the people of Bridgeville are going vegetarian for some reason. Not to worry, I'm sure they'll quickly return to their steak dinners. They always do."

Atticus had entered the kitchen almost silently, and they startled at his sudden appearance. He helped himself to some coffee, ruffling Fiona's hair as he moved to sit down.

"It's really snowing," Carsen remarked, tea in hand, nose pressed nervously against the window pane. "Is that normal?" Keaton gave a noncommittal sniff, looking unconcerned from his place at the sofa, wearing every sweater in the whole house. She took that as a yes. Frankie's answer was, as ever, more frank.

"Don't worry, the storm will let up. It always does." Frankie assured her, smiling confidently.

15

Just a Little While

The storm did not, in fact, let up. Inches of white powder continued to pile up on the ground, steadily climbing until it was pressed against the windows. Every few hours, Carsen would crawl across her bed to the window to check if it was still snowing, and when she inevitably found that it was, she would pinch herself to check that she was not dreaming it. The whole thing felt very dreamlike, after all - the chill washing over the blankets and dancing up her spine, the blur of snowflakes that were all that could be seen for miles.

The morning had a frosty start, as their old radiator came clunking to a halt. Carsen had never actually noticed the dull buzz of it until its absence made it conspicuous. At first, she couldn't place what the problem was, opting to go back to sleep in favor of believing the sound had been a part of a dream. She was rudely awoken by Keaton cursing so loudly that it sounded like he was right next to her. She stumbled out into the hallway to find everybody else having done the same thing.

Keaton came out of the bathroom, hair wet, eyes wild. "The hot water is out." He was barely able to get it out through his teeth chattering. Frankie gave a tiny laugh as she moved to get additional towels and blankets to swaddle him in, but it soon became clear that this was no laughing matter.

The heating in the whole house had gone out, they had no hot water, and they were effectively snowed in. The adults tried to keep things light for the girls, making it out to be a grand adventure, but the truth was that they were quickly running low on food, firewood, and, perhaps most importantly, blood.

Typically, every Friday, the butcher drove out as far as the railroad, where Atticus met him to receive all of the blood from that week's meat-cutting. Carsen wasn't clear on the particulars or on if the butcher knew what was happening or was just opting not to question the strange arrangement.

The phone had rung about noon that first day of freeze, startling everyone in the house. The house was pretty limited in the technology it had - a part of life when you had a developing witch in the house.

Carsen couldn't count the number of lightbulbs she'd burned out with a spark of uncontrolled emotion as a young girl. Before Carsen had arrived, Maddie had blown out three cell phones on three different occasions. In the end, they kept things simple - a television from the 1980s and a phone that looked like it would take its last call any day. It was an ancient thing, a rotary, and didn't run on electricity but magick. It only took calls that were life and death, because that was all the energy Carsen could spare. They had never heard it ring before. Atticus took the call, starting out cordial, but his face quickly became very serious.

"Yes, Jim, I understand that, but... Yes, that makes sense... Alright. Okay. Thanks for calling. I'll speak to you soon."

The phone returned to the cradle, leaving the room in total silence. All eyes were on Atticus, who looked as worried as Carsen had ever seen him.

Keaton gave a low hiss, and Carsen knew he had seen whatever the problem was.

"The butcher is snowed in," Atticus reported solemnly. "He can't come today. Probably not for the next few days."

Atticus lit the fire, recruiting the girls to carry in some of the firewood they had gathered that fall. Only sticks and pieces of tree that had already naturally fallen off were allowed to be collected; it was the only way that Fiona tolerated it. Fiona nearly tumbled into the room with her stack, carrying a log far too big for her six-year-old arms, and Frankie quickly relieved her of her duties. After Maddie had dumped hers in front of the fireplace place and returned to her seat, they all sat and waited. Too tight at the best of times, every inch of the room was currently being occupied. Keaton, Frankie, and Carsen, all crushed together on the loveseat, Fiona in Frankie's lap, and Maddie perched precariously on the loveseat's arm.

"What's your plan, Atticus? I know you have one," Frankie said.

"Yes, Atticus, what *is* your plan?" Keaton said darkly. He clearly disapproved of whatever harebrained scheme was about to be announced. Typically, Atticus didn't go for the harebrained option, but desperate times seemed like they were going to call for desperate measures.

"I'm going to have to go to town," Atticus said.

Immediately, a clamor of voices broke out. He raised his hand, and they quieted instantly. Carsen made a mental note to ask him how he did that when the circumstances were a little less dire.

"I know, I know, but it would appear that's our only option at this point. Keaton and I can't go without blood. We need food. We haven't fed since Wednesday. If there was another option, I'd take it."

There was a stunned silence. Carsen looked around the room. Keaton was positively fuming, jaw set so hard it looked like it could snap. Frankie was looking at her fingers, which were wringing each other near to death. Fiona and Maddie both looked deeply unsettled, though whether that was at the prospect of their adoptive father making such a perilous journey or at the tension in the room was hard to say. Probably both.

"I have a human heating charm I could use on you for the walk.

155

It *is* for humans, though, so I don't know how well it'll work on you, but it's worth a try for sure," Carsen piped up. She said it just as much to proffer the charm as she did to break the uncomfortable silence.

"And I could whip up some hot chocolate, for you to take with you." Frankie seemed relieved at the prospect of having something to do and was half out of her chair when Keaton erupted.

"So we're just letting this happen?" He rose from where he was squished between Frankie and Carsen and went to stand before Atticus, jaw jutted out, mouth a stern line. They were nearly chest to chest, and the tension between them sucked all the air from the room. It was easy to forget how tall Atticus was since he spent most of his time sitting at his desk, and the times he was standing, he slumped his shoulders a bit. Carsen had asked him about it once, and he had told her that when he first met Fiona, his height had terrified her and that by now, the purposeful shrinking had become merely a bad habit.

Even slumped now, he was half a head taller than Keaton and far more solid than the reedy blond. It dawned on Carsen that in all the time they had had together, Keaton had come to love Atticus in the same way that Fiona and Maddie did. Her heart broke for him, and she wished that there was another way out of this, any way to ease the agony she could feel emanating from his small, sad shoulders.

"There's no other option, Keaton," Atticus repeated, voicing her worry aloud. "This is just how it has to be."

156

Keaton whirled around and left the room. A moment later, they heard a door slam and knew he'd taken to the refuge of his bedroom.

"Now, how about that hot chocolate?" Atticus asked with a strained smile.

-

By the time they had gathered at the front door, collecting all their warmest sweaters and piling them onto Atticus, Keaton had collected himself and emerged from his room. He looked pale and drawn but said nothing as he watched Atticus struggle to wrap the last layer around himself.

Atticus finally managed to work the last button into place and then looked up at the rest of them, smiling like nothing out of the ordinary was happening. "I'll be back tomorrow morning. At the latest. Don't worry about a thing. I'll be perfectly fine." His voice was firm and steady and she wondered if secretly he was scared. He didn't seem to be.

He gave each of the girls a hug, Keaton a firm handshake with a long look, and was gone into the snow without another word.

-

It was the longest day Carsen had ever had. The adults tried their best to keep the girls occupied, their minds too busy to worry, but no matter how many games of Monopoly they played, the reality of the situation was still hanging in the air. The chill had long since settled deep into their bones, and the

157

little girls were wrapped in quilts at the kitchen table while the adults used pure willpower to still their chins from quivering. It took everything in Carsen not to bite her tongue off with her teeth chattering.

All of them could only pick at the sourdough bread Frankie had made. Fiona was the most herself of the group, painting pictures on her plate with her tomato bisque, using the bread as a paintbrush. She drew dozens of fat, thick snowflakes collecting onto a tiny house in the blood-red tomato. Carsen lost her appetite.

Maddie told Fiona she was tired at eight o'clock, a testament to her newfound maturity. The two traipsed off to bed, leaving the adults to sit at the kitchen table and keep vigil.

By half past one in the morning, it became clear that Keaton was going to need blood sooner than they thought. He had stood up to refill his cup of tea and nearly collapsed onto the floor. Frankie had snagged him at the last second, slotting him back into his seat with a grunt.

"I was worried this would happen," she muttered.

Keaton's skin was waxy-looking, his eyes rolling back into his head. His eyelids fluttered. Carsen reached out, eyes wide, and placed two fingers on his lifeline, trying desperately not to be tender.

"His lifeline is thin[16]. What do we do?" Carsen heard the way her voice cracked with panic, but couldn't spare the attention

158

to be embarrassed.

Frankie looked at her, sucking in her cheeks. "He needs blood. Soon."

Carsen stood and sidled up next to him, leaning down until they were practically nose to nose. "Keaton? Keaton, wake up. We need you."

It took a moment of them murmuring to him, tapping his wrists and cheeks and neck, but he came to full awareness in a rush.

"What's happening?" He gasped out, coming to in a sudden rush.

"I need you to do something for me," Carsen said tentatively.

This brought him fully into focus, and he sat up a bit. "What? What is it?"

It hurt her heart a bit, to see how quickly he roused himself at the idea that she needed him. She so fervently wanted to save this man, to help bring the life back into his cheeks.

She looked at him through her eyelashes, the way she always did when she was about to do something he wouldn't like, and pulled up her sleeve. White skin, with blue veins tracing the curves of her wrist. She examined it for a moment, dreading what would come next, and then offered it to him as easily as she had passed him the sugar for his tea that morning, a

159

moment that now felt a million miles away. She pressed her skin to his lips, trying not to shudder at his breath and the way it gusted across her flesh.

"No. Are you kidding? No!" He pushed her wrist away, gentle even in his anger. His eyes were flashing with indignation. The amount of vehemence in this response gave her a little bit of comfort, even though he sagged a little after the protestations.

"I trust you," she said as though it was the most obvious thing in the world. She clenched her fist, and the veins and tendons pulsed with the movement.

He swallowed hard and flinched away from her, looking betrayed. "Why are you doing this to me?"

"Because you can't drink Frankie's blood. I'm sure she'd offer. But since she can't, I'm afraid you'll have to make do with mine."

He looked pleadingly at Frankie, but she pointedly looked away, the tension in her jaw a clear agreement but unwilling to put words to it.

"I can wait. I'm fine. We don't need to do this now. This could be over any time, and you could have risked this for nothing."

Carsen's nostrils flared, and she reached out faster than she'd moved in ages and grabbed his hand. She held it up for his examination. "Does this look like you can wait?" she

160

snapped. It was shaking, quivering in such earnest that he was embarrassed by it. He yanked his hand away and hid it behind him.

They said nothing for a moment, just stood in an angry silence that felt uncomfortable and unfamiliar.

"You're being cruel," he said, voice raw, eyes reddening.

"She's being practical," Frankie said firmly. "We've no choice in the matter, so get it over with and bite her, would you? I can't stand much more waiting."

"You won't hurt me," Carsen said confidently.
   "What makes you think that? Did you *see* it?" he asked disparagingly, glowering up at her.

"No. I just trust you."

Keaton was quiet for what felt like a decade. Finally, he swallowed hard and looked just to the right of Carsen's face. "Fine."

"I'll give you two some privacy," Frankie murmured, slipping from the room like a ghost, entirely un-Frankie-like. Carsen spared a moment to wonder what she thought of the whole thing, whether she was jealous that it wasn't her, if she regretted it on his behalf or her own.

They heard a door close upstairs, and then it was just them in the kitchen. Neither of them said anything for quite a while,

Carsen waiting for him to make a move and Keaton waiting for her to change her mind. The decision was made when Keaton went yet another shade whiter and slid down in his chair.

"Okay, this is ridiculous. Where do you want to bite? What is easiest?"

He glared at her. "Your neck. Haven't you ever seen a movie? Monsters like me love to chew on poor innocent human necks."

She couldn't tell if he had said this to frighten her off, but it did make her stomach flip a little. She took a deep breath.

"Okay." She tilted her head and shook her hair out, ignoring Keaton's scandalized gasp as she carefully tucked it over her shoulder. She pushed the remainder behind her ear.

"I'm ready. Go ahead." She closed her eyes.

She sat there like a stone for what felt like forever, just breathing in and out, focusing on the way that her lungs felt as they expanded and deflated in that steady rhythm. Then, before she knew what was happening, there was a resigned sigh, and he was biting her.

If she'd been expecting it to hurt (to be honest, she hadn't let herself think about it too much), she was wrong. There was no pain at all, just the sensation of a dull warmth at the side of her neck and Keaton gingerly holding her head steady, a hand on each side of her face like she was made of glass and would break if she wasn't handled with the utmost care. Quite suddenly, the warmth turned into a flame, the world fell clear away from her, and all she could think about was the desperate heat at her neck. It still wasn't quite painful, though. Somewhere between pain and pleasure, if she was being honest. It was over before she could fully wrap her head around it.

Carsen could hear a distant rummaging and felt a bandaid being placed on her neck. She could've sworn she felt a tiny kiss on it, but that could have been her imagination.

She was struck with a keen yearning, a desperate wishing for more. She wanted his lips on her, whether they were biting her or not.

She could dimly hear someone calling her name. They sounded concerned, and she tried to get her mouth to work so she could tell whoever it was not to worry that she'd truly never felt better.

"Carsen!" Keaton was shaking her now, looking stricken. His cheeks had the slightest tinge of pink to them (Carsen breathed again), but the effect was diminished by the miserable look on his face.

She shook her head, the daze drifting away. She watched it leave with a bit of sadness in her stomach but only allowed herself a moment to wallow. Someone was asking her something.

163

"Are you feeling alright? Did I take too much? You look a bit pale. I can have Frankie get you something to drink, I think there's some apple juice left from Fiona's harvest..."

"I'm fine, Keaton. I just need to stay seated for a bit. Really, what's the point of cohabitating with a human if I'm not also your cute little emotional support blood bag?" She was going for light-hearted, but Keaton's brow knotted up, and he was quiet for a moment.

"I'm sorry...Too soon?" she asked, reaching a pale hand out to him. He caught it and held it hard. She was always surprised at how soft he was. Vampires were meant to be hard and cold and aloof, and he was only slightly cool to the touch. Still, a bit distant, but not like before. She hadn't seen this look on his face in a long time.

"No, it's okay. It's just... I never wanted to do that. I don't like having to be a monster with you."

Carsen felt her stomach drop out. "None of that, mister. I did what *I* wanted to do, nothing more, nothing less."

"Yes, but-"

"No buts! What was I supposed to do, watch someone I love waste away? You were almost green!" She was a little angry now, wondering if she shouldn't encourage him to talk to Atticus about speaking to somebody about his self-esteem issues. Keaton didn't respond. She refocused on him and saw he had a strange look on his face along with a bright, sparkling flush high in his cheeks.

"What?" she asked, cocking her head.

"You love me?" he asked, awestruck.

Her eyes widened. She *had* said that, hadn't she? "Oh, I..."

Carsen thought about Frankie, the way that from the first day she'd come through those gates, she had made her feel safe and steady and like she was at home. That was love, no doubt about it. It had been instant and easy. Keaton's love had been slower, a creeping thing that had gotten into the roots of her without her even noticing before it was intertwined with her every fiber.

But it was love. Suddenly, she was certain of it. She thought of the tiny freckle in his left eye, the way that when he got tired or angry, his drawl got a little thicker, how he read even more than she did, the way he gloated when he won at Scrabble.

"Yes, I suppose I do." A tear came unbidden, dripping down her cheek, falling into the line of her smile.

Keaton looked like he was the sun, glowing in a way she had never seen him do before. "Could I..." he looked unsure, leaning forward like he was teetering on the precipice of something, and suddenly she was pulling him forward by the lapel of his corduroy jacket, and they were pressing against one another. She had imagined him hard, but he was as soft as she was and nearly as pliant. His skin was cold, and she took a deep breath, feeling like she was about to dive underwater.

"I love you too," he whispered. Even as they were kissing, even as she felt his fangs graze her bottom lip, she felt him smile under her.

"By the way," he said, in a voice that was trying for casual but overshot it by a wide margin. "You tasted a little weird. You might be anemic. When the snow clears up you should make an appointment with the doctor."

Carsen froze for a moment before twisting to look at Keaton's face to see if he was serious.

He was.

Carsen started to laugh, shaking with it.

"What?" Keaton said, looking disconcerted. This was clearly not the reaction he had been anticipating.

"Nothing," she choked out, still giggling. "Nothing at all."

He reached out a hand, and she took his cold fingers in hers. Keaton led her back to Frankie, likely with no idea of the soaring feeling in her stomach.

–

"Do you hear that?" Frankie's head cocked, eyes distant.

"Hear what?" Keaton asked, crunching on a burned piece of

166

toast. Carsen had never noticed before, but Keaton was a stress eater, and he'd spent that morning steadily working his way through their last loaf of bread with only a little shame.

"It's an engine, I think. Coming this way?" Frankie stood up and went to the front door. Opting not to open it due to the bitter cold, she peered through the peephole.

"Is this thing supposed to actually work or is it just a decoration? I can't see anything," she groused.

Keaton rose to his feet. "I hear it, too."

He strode confidently to the door and swung it open. There, puttering in their front yard having shoved a path through the snow seemingly through sheer will, was a gigantic tank of a Jeep.

"What the-?" Frankie whispered.

Carsen could see Atticus's rail-thin figure appear from the passenger's seat and craned her neck to see who was driving.

A curly head of long dark hair popped out from the driver's side. "Did someone order groceries?"

Zahra, the town librarian, emerged from the vehicle, looking fashionable and unbothered by the wind and wet in her simple trench coat, toting what was without a doubt, a blood bag.

16

She

"Us magickal creatures have to stick together, don't you think?" Zahra was a rush of activity, somehow able to put milk in the fridge while simultaneously starting a kettle brewing.

"You're-?" Maddie was oscillating wildly between being standoffish and cagey about their visitor (reasonably so, Carsen thought, as in the entire time Carsen had lived there not a single soul had come to call) and being starstruck by Zahra. It was hard not to be.

She was tall and lean, vaguely cat-like from her figure to the shape of her eyes. She wore the kind of outfit that made Carsen look down at her thrice-repaired overalls and vow to try harder from now on.

"How did you know that we were magick?" Keaton demanded. He was even more wary than Maddie.

"What do you mean, how did I know?" she demanded right back, turning to Atticus.

The older man grimaced. "Everybody, Zahra is my...special friend."

Carsen's jaw dropped open so hard that it clicked. Frankie hid a smile in the corner of her mouth. Keaton guffawed, a sound so full of delight and wonder that Carsen couldn't help but be pleased too.

Atticus was sheepish, explaining to Zahra how he had been meaning to tell them but just hadn't gotten around to it, while Zahra appraised him with a fond look in her eyes. The girls were wide-eyed and clearly uncomprehending, and Carsen made a note to explain things to them later. She smirked to herself, thinking of that day in town and the hickey on Atticus's neck.

His gigantic stack of library books made even more sense now.

–

The sunlight was just barely offsetting the chill of the winter wind on Carsen's skin. She watched their three shadows as they walked along, her and Frankie with strands of hair whipping about and Keaton just an outline of coat, pants, and shoes, a headless figure. She had thought it was a myth that vampires couldn't be seen in the mirror (for a while, she thought vampires were a myth, period). It turns out it was

169

true, something about the way that the light refracts off of them. Keaton always subtly asked Frankie after eating if there was something on his face. For his part, Atticus somehow had mastered keeping himself perfectly clean and orderly without the help of his reflection.

She stared down at their feet: three sets of snow boots, one pair perilously close to being untied. Carsen subtly jerked a finger at Frankie's shoelaces, and they retied and tightened. Frankie kept walking, chatting about this and that, utterly unaware. One side of Keaton's mouth quirked up, but he said nothing.

She listened absently to Frankie talk at them, her usual stream of pleasant chatter ("Isn't the snow lovely! Winter has always been my favorite season, what about you, Carsen? Keaton, I know you say you hate it, but I think you secretly like it even though you get cold.") and tried to identify the feeling in her chest. It was a kind of tightness, not unpleasant, a little warm. It felt like the night two days before Christmas, or when you wake up in the middle of the night and know you have hours left to sleep.

She was perfectly content.

–

In retrospect, Carsen had known on some level that they wouldn't be able to dance around things forever. It was too much hanging in the air, too heavy a meaning to words said and touches under the kitchen table. But still, she was surprised when Frankie brought it up.

The werewolf had been making a strange level of eye contact with her from the moment she had made it down to the breakfast table that morning.

"I have to show you something in my room." Her voice was furtive, eyes searching the room for potential eavesdroppers. She found none, given that Atticus was locked in his office, presumably writing yet another one of those mysterious letters that they now knew went to Zahra, and the girls were playing outside in the last of the melting snow.

"Huh?" Keaton was still waking up, his hair sticking up on one side. He groggily rubbed at his eyes and looked at Frankie like she was speaking gibberish. The jam from his toast was all over his face. Carsen reached out with a napkin.

"I need to show you both something in my room," Frankie explained.

Carsen and Keaton nodded and followed, knowing it was useless to deny Frankie anything. They both always gave her anything she wanted in the end.

Once inside, Frankie shut the door and leaned on it, eyes flicking between the two of them. "I think we all should fuck." Her voice was utterly calm and rational, as though she was simply putting in her requests for the groceries that week rather than blowing up the dancing around each other that the trio had been doing for months.

Carsen and Keaton both avoided eye contact with each other,

171

opting for the ground or the view through the window. A long, awkward silence followed.

"Nothing? Really? I think it's time we talk about this, don't you guys?" Frankie looked at them. Both had dropped jaws, gawping like a fish out of water.

"I'm not-" Carsen stuttered.

"Don't know what-" Keaton mumbled.

"In case you've forgotten, I do have super senses," Frankie said simply, leaning casually against the door that she'd been guarding. When all she received was blank looks, she scoffed. "Really, people! Concentrate!" Frankie looked like she couldn't decide whether she wanted to laugh or cry.

"Carsen, I can hear your heartbeat increase every time Keaton gets within five feet of you. And you, Keaton, are simply obvious. Anyone with two working eyes can see what you feel."

Carsen said nothing, looking at Frankie imploring her to stop, please stop this, leave this elephant in the room alone.

Keaton made an inelegant 'pshaw' noise. Frankie raised an eyebrow.

"Keaton, I hear you at night. I hear what you say, and I smell what you do, and you're not fooling anyone, especially not me. Don't you think it would just be easier if we talked about this?"

It was lucky that Keaton couldn't blush, but Carsen could, and the blood rushed to her face so quickly that she felt a bit faint. Frankie was going scorched earth on them all. No matter what happened next, nothing would be the same when they left that room.

"Frankie, I-" Carsen started.

"Well, what do you propose?" Keaton interrupted stiffly, ignoring Carsen entirely. His spine was ramrod straight, and he looked a bit like a soldier preparing to storm a battlefield.

"I already said what I 'propose,'" she said, all air quotes and glee. "We should fuck. All three of us."

Carsen and Keaton were absolutely silent.

A thousand images were flying through Carsen's head. Keaton painting a portrait of her, being overly generous with her features, and then asking if he could keep it ("I'd like to be able to...see you whenever I'd like," he said shyly). *An angel. He had to be an angel.*

Frankie lying next to her, smelling like lemongrass.[17] *She means everything to me.*

Both of them at the breakfast table, Frankie keeping up a steady stream of chatter even as the toast she was eating entered her mouth. Keaton, barely disguising his pure delight at the proceedings.

How could she not want them both?

They both agreed at the same moment.

17

Loverboy

The three of them were all curled up in bed after dinner, legs tangled, Frankie's braid laying across Keaton's chest, so long that it brushed Carsen's cheek on his other side. Carsen smiled at the thought of them all being connected, even afterward.

"Have you two…done this before?" She'd been wanting to ask the question for weeks but had been scared of the answer. She was still a little anxious but figured it was better the devil you knew.

Frankie and Keaton looked at each other and grinned.

"Once or twice," Keaton confirmed. "You know, Frankie got here a little more than two years ago. I was hesitant at first, just like I was with you."

"Is that what you call hesitant?" Carsen scoffed, laughing a bit.

Keaton ignored her snipe and continued. "But you know how it is with Frankie. You're around her for more than twenty minutes, and you can't help but fall in love with her."

Carsen hummed her agreement, tugging a bit at Frankie's braid.

Frankie giggled, and the other two melted. "Stop it! You guys are making me blush."

"Good," Keaton said, kissing her on the forehead. "There was this one time, during Yule last year… I could show you, Carsen. Frankie, should I show her?"

Frankie sat up, eyes wide with excitement. "Yes, Keaton, let's show her."

Carsen was wide-eyed too, but for a different reason. "What on earth are you talking about-oh." She suddenly remembered what Atticus had done her very first day. *We have the ability to share a memory with only a touch.*

"Yes, oh." Keaton was usually so gentle, but his smile looked sharp, his longing heavy in the air. "May I?" He and Frankie were both upright now, eyes intent on her.

Carsen took a split second to think, imagining what she might see. Imagining them watching her see.

That decided it. "You may," she whispered. Keaton's cold fingers were on her in half a heartbeat.

–

"Tis the season, I suppose," Keaton gasped, thrusting against her.

"I'm Jewish," Frankie choked out, barely able to form a sentence. Her skin, burning to begin with, was bordering on volcanic.

"Well, Hanukkah already passed, love," he murmured, dragging a cold finger across her burning cheek.

He ran his fingertips through the ridges and valleys of her scar tissue. Her skin was so warm against his cold hands that it felt like he was inside of a fire and somehow miraculously escaping a burn. Even as he was kissing her, he knew it was far too much to ask. He pressed himself into her too-warm body, waiting for his wings to melt.

Outside of all of it, somewhere far away, Carsen could dimly feel two sets of hands on her, one burning hot and one ice cold. They were in her hair, on her neck, at her waist. One of them was kissing her, and she could feel the fangs, just the slightest bit catching at her lip. She tasted blood and hoped it wasn't Keaton kissing her. The temptation might be too much for him.

"The way you're looking at me.[18] I feel like you might eat me," Frankie growled, looking like she wanted desperately to be eaten.

"I'd really like to," Keaton said, looking up at her from where he was sitting between her legs.

Carsen pulled out from the vision very suddenly, soaked in sweat and breathing hard.

"You're blushing," Keaton teased, smoothing a thumb over her cheek. Carsen shuddered at the touch, a shiver running up her spine.

Frances poked him in the ribs, and he squirmed away. That was another thing Carsen loved about Keaton, how a hundred-some-year-old vampire could be ticklish. "Don't tease her. If you had any blood running through your veins, you'd be blushing too," Frankie said with a laugh.

"I wasn't teasing. I quite like it. It's very attractive, the both of you looking at me all red in the face."

Frankie rolled her eyes at this before turning to Carsen, flipping her from her side to her back, and kissing her neck fiercely.

"Are you going to bite me?" Carsen whispered, feeling unearthly.

"When I'm not a wolf, I can bite you plenty. As much as I want." Frankie was breathing a little hard, tiny droplets of sweat creating a halo over her hairline and making the short hair around her forehead even curlier. "We can do whatever we want."

Carsen warmed even more at the thought.

-

In the early hours, Carsen carefully extracted herself from the pile of arms and legs and blankets, and padded her way to the bathroom, counting on her socks to keep her steps quiet enough to not wake Keaton. Frankie she didn't have to worry about. She slept like a log. In the night, they had switched positions, Frankie moving to the middle to provide warmth to both of them. She had done the job well, and even in the middle of a snowy December, the sweater of Keaton's and the underwear of Frankie's that she wore had kept her body perfectly warm.

She stared at herself in the mirror, looking to see if she looked any different than she had yesterday morning. She felt different. It was only right that there should be something in her eyes or the flush of her cheeks to reflect it.

But she looked the same as she always did, with mussed brown hair and pale skin. The only thing out of the ordinary was the rows of bite marks crisscrossing her throat. She stepped closer to the mirror to examine them.

She could tell with ease which ones were from Frankie and which ones belonged to Keaton. The vampire fangs left two light indents, the way she pictured a snake would. He had been so gentle that his teeth hadn't even broken skin, simply leaving her with two small bruises littered across her collarbone; he had seemed particularly interested in that area. Frankie's calling card looked like regular bite marks, the slightest bit

179

red and raised, full circles of teeth, just under her ear, where her jaw met her neck.

It was so very them. Keaton's fervent belief in her delicacy. Frankie's knowledge of her needs while also her ability to separate them from her strength. She appreciated them both, each in their own way, and loved them even more.

The morning grew later, and Frankie and Keaton awoke, laying there in the pleasant silence, all quiet parallel breaths that puffed across her from both sides, one warm and one cool. Carsen was in the middle now, having usurped the coveted spot after her morning bathroom venture. One effect of taking the middle was that both of her lovers had the opportunity to inspect her. And they were taking full advantage.

"What are these?" Frankie asked, playing with the ridge of Carsen's ear.

"I'm more curious about this one," Keaton commented, poking the side of her nose where a small stud gleamed in the morning light.

Carsen wiggled her nose at the sensation and sniffed. Keaton patted the tip of her nose in apology.

"That one's an opal, the one in my nose. It increases psychic connections. And that one," she said, tilting her head to poke her cartilage piercing into Frankie's hand, "is black tourmaline for protection."

"And the purple one? In the middle here?" Keaton tapped her right ear.

"Amethyst. For pain." Carsen instantly wondered if she had spoiled the mood. Those thoughts were banished when both Frankie and Keaton curled into her, enveloping her in their arms in a perfect circle of caring and love.

18

Sweater Weather

Every day was a new success for Carsen. She had been able to go without her cane for several weeks, something that was exciting to her not because of any disdain for the cane, which had carried her countless miles, but due to what it meant for her diminished pain levels. She had coached Maddie into producing fire with one finger without so much as a singed eyebrow (far better than she'd achieved her first few go-rounds). And perhaps most delightfully, with each passing hour, she was falling deeper, more and more blissfully in love with not one but *two* magickal creatures.

Her only worry was that she might inconvenience them out of love with her.

One of Carsen's bad habits was that she would get immensely absorbed in a task and allow her blood sugar to drop into a pit that would leave her sweaty and shaking, unable to get a full sentence out. It usually wasn't a *problem*. A bit embarrassing, sure, but still something she would apologize for and then handle in private.

Keaton didn't seem to agree with that approach.

She had been so absorbed in lesson planning for Maddie (Yule was just around the corner, and she was excited to teach the young werewolf all about the ceremony that marked the longest night of the year) that she had forgotten to eat all day.

When she had looked up from the lesson plan, she had felt the quicksand sinking feeling and struggled to her feet. She moved as though through molasses to the kitchen, made eye contact with Keaton, the sole occupant, and then wavered, nearly collapsing where she stood. Keaton was up in a flash, grabbing her gently and placing her in a seat near the stove. He could smell it in her, and his eyes flashed with worry.

"I don't know why you didn't just fucking say something! I'd have brought you breakfast, or lunch, or a snack, or anything else on earth that you wanted," he snapped, holding out a flask of apple juice.

Carsen grimaced. Keaton never swore. He was too much of an old-fashioned Southern gentleman for that. If the shaking of his hands wasn't enough to indicate his anger, this newfound and uncharacteristically foul mouth was.

She didn't say anything, just begrudgingly accepted the drink.

He glowered at her, and she shifted in her spot so as to

183

distribute the disdain being directed at her.

"Is it fun for you, terrifying everyone around you?" he demanded, not letting up.

This was so sudden an attack that her jaw dropped a little. It took a moment for her to gather herself to answer. "No." she said softly. "it's just... you know, sometimes when you're the only one who needs things, you just get tired of asking."

It was something that had been eating at her for some time, almost as long as she'd been in the house. It was hard not to think like that, living surrounded by magickal creatures who were so much stronger, faster, *better* than her. She could, what, float a few books around? Stir up a tincture if need be? How could that compare to them? Even little Fiona could impact the growth patterns of the entire ecosystem of their backyard.

His hands stilled at their place at the stove. He'd been making angry pops rise from the stovetop, heat turned far too high, and when he turned it down, the fire puttered out completely.

"Have I ever made you feel like you can't-"

"No, of course not. It's stupid. I'm sorry." She tried to push up from her seat at the table but found gravity and his hand on her shoulder preventing her from doing so.

"Please don't be sorry. I hate it when you're sorry." He had softened significantly, now just looking tired. That was the thing with Keaton. Anger usually just meant he was feeling an emotion he wasn't comfortable with.

She looked at him. As his gaze came to rest on her face, she became acutely, self-consciously aware of just how worse for wear she really was. The shadows under her eyes were like bruises, standing out all the more starkly because of the way the color had been leeched from her skin by the fall and winter months. Her hair was a knotted mess. *She* was a mess. In a way that was more instinctual than anything else, he pushed some of it from her eyes, tucking it behind her ear.

"Look, I'm sorry, Carsen began. "As you have said so many times, I'm just a human. And humans need things. Like sleep. And food and water. I suppose in a lot of ways it's a bit like keeping a pet. And I've been a bad pet owner to myself lately. Won't happen again."

"I never said 'just a human.'"

It was almost a murmur, so quiet she had to lean in a bit to hear him. "What?" She wanted to hear it again. To hear him mean it. Her stomach twisted as she waited for him to decide if he was up to repeating it.

"I never said you were just a human. I don't think you're 'just' anything."

Carsen almost gasped aloud with the feeling of hearing it, but she swallowed it just in time. She sat in silence for a second, simply digesting the words she had longed to hear her whole

185

life.

"Thank you," she settled on. "I appreciate that." And with that, overcome and panicked, Carsen ran out the door without another word.

He found her outside, her breath coming in puffs into the biting air. The chill had frozen the tears into her eyelashes, and she was sure she looked a bit unearthly. She certainly felt that way.

"It's too cold for you out here. You can't rush out without a coat," he muttered, wrapping her in his sweater. She let him, trying to resist breathing in his scent but finding herself unable, and maybe unwilling, to avoid it.

Keaton stepped back to examine his handiwork and stared.

Carsen shifted self-consciously. "What?"

"The way you look in my sweater," Keaton answered, drawing closer. He sighed, not a little dreamily, pupils dilated. "I'm still a man, Carsen. Just a man with fangs."

Even without a coat, Carsen was suddenly filled with warmth.

Atticus informed her over oatmeal the next morning that they would be doing some work on the tincture. She blinked,

186

having almost forgotten about one of the main reasons she had come here.

"Alright, that sounds great! But...where are we going to work?" She didn't want to be rude, but she'd seen his office more than once, and there was scarcely enough room to spin around with your arms out, much less do any sort of potion work.

He smiled knowingly. "Not anywhere in the house, don't worry. I have a place we can go."

She hummed her agreement, then turned to see Keaton staring intently at her. She cocked her head.

"Is there something on my face?" she asked, rubbing at the corners of her mouth self-consciously. *Serves me right for eating the last of the jam.*

Keaton shook his head like a wet dog, as though coming back from somewhere very far away. "No, nothing. Sorry." He bent his head over the newspaper that had been delivered two weeks ago and pretended to read it as though it was the most fascinating thing on earth. She rolled her eyes. *Whatever.* She had bigger fish to fry.

–

The place turned out to be a beaten-down shed about ten yards into the woods behind the house. Carsen had hesitated before entering because the moment Atticus opened the door, there had been a terrible creaking sound that made her think the

187

whole thing would come down, as well as an awful musty smell whooshing from the doorway. Atticus had forged forward undeterred though, as though he wasn't being choked by the mildewed air, and so she had forced herself to follow suit, breathing strictly through her mouth.

"So," he said, clapping his hands to indicate it was time to begin. "My thinking is that your condition has something to do with your immune system. Some sort of overactive white cells being activated by your magick, or the electric pulses in your blood that happen when you do your magick."

Carsen nodded. This was about where she and all the magick doctors she'd previously seen had come to as well. She was a little nervous that this was all he had come up with in all this time.

"So what we do from there is relatively easy. We imbue your white cells with the same electricity as comes from your magick, consistently, on a semi-regular basis. At the end of treatment, they should have become properly acquainted with your magick's signature, and the white blood cells won't have such an intense reaction when you're casting."

Carsen nearly laughed aloud. "You're going to electrocute me? What happened to the tincture?"

Carsen had expected she'd just have to swallow something terrible and feel a bit (or a lot) ill for a few days. Not sustained pain enacted purposely "on a semi-regular basis" by someone close to her.

188

"I'm not electrocuting *you*, just your cells," Atticus said.

"Will it hurt?" she demanded.

"Probably a bit. But if it works, it could fix you forever."

If. Her least favorite word, one she had heard dozens of times from people with a slightly callous scientific mind, men like Atticus. She had never seen this side of him before, the one with the curious twinkle in his eye, the one giddy with the thought of progress. It made her stomach squirm to think that this version of him had been inside him all along. This was the Atticus that Keaton had known, the reason he was so wary of him, why he still didn't trust him fully even now after living with him for who knows how many years.

"Can I have some time to think about it?" she asked, staring at her feet.

Atticus furrowed his thick brows but nodded nonetheless. "But don't wait long. The sooner we start, the more effective it will be."

-

That night, as Frankie lit the Hannukkah lights and then moved on to the Shabbat candles, Carsen watched the way her frame was silhouetted by the candlelight. She watched the other woman's reflection in the window and wondered about magick. She had been very confident in what it was - she was a witch, after all. Magick wasn't just what she *did*. It was who she *was*.

But something about the way that the people in this house made her feel that it was mystical, and it wasn't just their fangs and snouts. It was love. The idea made her stomach twist. She imagined perfect Frankie and beautiful Keaton together next to a small, withering, crumpled-up thing. *This isn't going to last forever. Enjoy it while you can.*

As Frankie recalled the miracle, Carsen hoped for one of her own.

19

Cello Suite No. 6 in D Major

C arsen didn't shut her eyes for even a second that night. All she could think about were images of Frankenstein and being struck by lightning. Haunted and exhausted, she came to Atticus the next morning looking half-dead. Even more than her actually undead housemates.

She knocked nervously on the door, but it swung open immediately as though he had been waiting for her. She stepped inside, stomach a mess.

"Atticus-"

"Carsen, I wanted to apologize," Atticus interrupted before she could even begin. "I thought it over last night, and I have asked far too much of you. As I'm sure you've heard, sometimes I can get swept away in my own interests, and this seems to have been one of those times. We will find another way."

Carsen positively sagged with relief. She wanted nothing more than to feel better, but even she had her limits.

Yule came with a flurry of excitement. They decorated a pine tree, one on the tree line that was closest to the house.

Carsen was quite pleased with her gifts for everyone. She had a crystal for each person in the house; Keaton got sodalite for communication and self-expression, Frankie a rose quartz ring for love, Fiona a pair of moss agate earrings for communing with nature, a prehnite necklace to encourage self-love and psychic connection for Maddie, and some selenite for peace and self-knowledge for Atticus.

Everybody had done their gift swapping early in the morning, and then after breakfast, as the girls and Atticus played with their new toys, the three of them retreated to Frankie's room. They always went to Frankie's room - it had the biggest bed, most likely to fit the three of them comfortably.

In the end, Carsen's Yule was quite spectacular.

Frankie had handmade a recipe book for her, all of them garlic-free recipes, with beautiful watercolors of each dish in the margins. Carsen gazed at her, wildly impressed. "Looks like Keaton isn't the only artist in the house."

Frankie blushed at this but ignored it and waved a hand at Keaton, who, if vampires could blush, was blushing too. "Wait till you see what he did."

"It's not much," he muttered, mock glaring at Frankie. "I'd thank you not to get her hopes up."

Carsen playfully cocked her head. "Too late now. Let's see it."

After a moment's hesitation, Keaton pulled a knobby pair of green mittens from underneath where he sat. Carsen gaped at him.

"I taught myself to knit. They're sort of awful. I'd understand if you didn't want to wear them. I just figured, you know, it's the thought that counts, and—" she interrupted his nervous ramble with a huge hug.

He practically purred under her embrace.

Keaton, it turned out, was full of secret talents. That night, while they ate Christmas dinner, he entertained them with concerto after concerto on his cello. The low sound was nearly human, echoing the house and wrapping them all in it. Carsen marveled at how fast his fingers moved, knowing they must be freezing; Keaton got so cold at the best of times. Even now, he wore knit fingerless gloves, black ones of Carsen's own design.

After Keaton played the final note of one of his favorite pieces, Cello Suite No. 6 in D Major by Bach, Atticus tapped a knife on his glass and stood.

"To a less eventful spring," Atticus said solemnly, raising his glass with a twinkle in his eye.

193

III

Spring

20

In Two

Carsen woke up from a nightmare of her mother dying violently right in front of her and immediately started sobbing. She felt her heart going in her chest, thumping furiously and unevenly, and wondered if she should be worried for her health.

Big palms and long, cold spindly fingers held her face. "What is it? What's wrong?" Keaton asked.

She hiccuped and sighed in relief. *A dream. Just a dream.* "Did I ever tell you what happened when I left?"

-

"Why would you go? We have everything you could possibly need right here!" Carsen's mother looked stricken, completely out of herself.

"I can't be here anymore. They might have a cure, and even if they don't - I'm tired of being trapped in the bedroom I grew up in, Mom. I can't live and die here. There's a whole world out there."

"It's not safe," her mother pleaded.

Carsen wanted to scream. "People live out in the real world every day, and they're perfectly safe. This? This isn't the real world; it's some strange manufactured facsimile. And it's one that holds every bad memory I've ever made."

"It holds every good one, too," her mom said defensively.

Carsen softened. "You're right, it does. But think of all the ones out there we could be making but can't because we stay stuck in this quicksand place."

And suddenly, she was off, running down a cobblestone street, suitcase flying furiously behind her in a desperate attempt to keep up. She hadn't moved this fast in years, the anger and hurt blocking out all the pain. She thought of her cane, folded up in her bag, and how she'd need to rely on it for at least a week after this escapade. She thought of the bookshelf in her bedroom and all the books she'd been meaning to get to that she was leaving behind. She thought of the look on her mother's face as she left.

She was so tired of thinking.

She passed a group of tourists who were staring and pointing at her and her floating suitcase. Good. Let them have a magickal Salem moment. The place was magick, after all.

Only so much blood can be spilled on the ground without it being so.

-

"That was brave of you," Keaton said, running his fingers through her tangled hair. He found a knot and began to work at it. They had moved to the living room so as not to wake Frankie and sat on the loveseat, eyelids heavy in the moonlight.

"I think it was cruel of me," Carsen countered, tipping her head back from its position on his lap to look at him.

"It's not cruel to make decisions that benefit you. It's the adult thing to do."

She was quiet a moment, considering this. "You really think so?"

"I know so. Trust me. I've been alive a very long time. I know what cruelty looks like. You could never even touch it, darling."

She smiled and closed her eyes.

-

There was something about seeing somebody first thing in the morning that meant you couldn't help but fall in love with them. The way that Frankie was more grouchy the first five minutes of the day than any of the rest of it. The image

199

of Keaton reading the newspaper while eating his toast and having his morning blood. She loved the softness of them, the bleary frame of early hours.

She wondered if they were charmed by anything she did. She doubted it.

They sat at the kitchen table, the three of them and Atticus, eating breakfast in companionable silence. Sometimes, it felt like all they did was sit and eat toast in each other's presence. She found that she was alright with that.

"Carsen, I have another…option for us to try. Would you like to do that today, or-" Atticus asked.

"Yes. Today, yes."

Carsen was feeling the pang of running out of time nearly as stoutly as she felt the throb in her hip bones. She could not go back empty-handed. She wouldn't.

Keaton and Frankie were looking at each other, doing that thing where they had a silent conversation with their eyes, but Carsen didn't care what they thought. They had no idea what the pain was like, the feeling of desperation, the drive to try anything, even something that made things worse for a while in a wild attempt to make the slightest bit of difference to your own destiny.

"Alright then. I'll go get it." Atticus was clearly also aware of the discussion happening solely through eyelid flutters, but he was also ignoring it. She liked that about Atticus. His ability to rise above things and not let them eat at him.

"Carse, are you sure?" Frankie asked as soon as Atticus left the room. Her eyes were pained, as though questioning Carsen's decisions cost her something.

Carsen appreciated that but still found herself irritated. Probably the pain. It made her unpleasant. Yet another reason to persist.

"I am absolutely completely 1000% sure."

Atticus had returned (had he run? Was he that worried she'd change her mind? Did they all think she was that weak? Her heart ached.) holding a vial of amber liquid. It looked like the color of Frankie's eyes, and that relaxed her.

"Are you ready?" Atticus asked, eyes a practiced vacant gaze, all his stress visible in the fold between his eyebrows.

Carsen smiled wanly and nodded. She took the shot glass of liquid he handed her and downed it in one gulp. Without warning, sleep washed over her like a wave, and she was gone.

She slept for three days, coming to in the vaguest sense a few times to find Frankie or Keaton, or both, standing watch.

When she came to the final time, they were both there.

"Atticus!" Keaton yelled, panicked, leaning down to touch her face. Frankie sobbed.

Atticus rocketed into the room. "Carsen? Carsen. Tell me exactly how you feel. Every detail."

Carsen was scared to close her eyes ever again, but she did, if only for a moment, to scan her body. Pain. The usual, and the stiffness that comes from sleeping for days. Her eyes opened again. "It hurts. Nothing different."

The room was silent for a moment. Carsen refused to allow herself to cry, focusing on the needles stabbing her spine to center herself.

"When do we try the next thing?" she asked.

21

Upstate

"Carsen! Carsen, wake up!" The words were hissed from her doorway in the dead of night, and she was quite certain she had two-thirds of a heart attack as a result.

Absolutely staggering with sleep, she clumsily made her way to the hallway.

"What is it, what's wrong?" It came out in a mumbled rush, her words all strung together like the Christmas lights they hadn't yet taken down.

Keaton stood there in his dressing gown, starry-eyed and hair mussed up. "Come look at this." He was beaming with excitement, looking exactly like Fiona always did when one of her plants had grown their first sprout.

She followed him out the back door to the porch, wondering what on earth this could possibly be about.

"Look," he breathed.

Five deer were traipsing through the yard, quiet as can be.

Carsen stood there speechless for a moment, watching them cross. They fit right in here, really. There was something otherworldly about them, the way that their feet barely skimmed the ground as they walked.

She felt herself yawn but barely noticed it until she heard Keaton's abashed "I'm sorry I woke you. You should go back to sleep."

"No, no, don't be silly. I'm glad you came to get me. Just look at them. They're so beautiful! Look at the cute little spots on their backs."

He nodded solemnly as though the cute little spots were a life-or-death matter. "They have the most gigantic eyes. Bore right into you. It's like they're staring down your soul and weighing it for heaven or hell."

Carsen raised an eyebrow at this unusually verbose answer. "I didn't know you were such a big fan of deer."

He smiled then, and she could see a glint of fang in the moonlight. "I don't know if *fan* is the right word. Maybe connoisseur. I've drained quite a lot of them in my time."

She worked mightily to subdue the shiver that went down her spine. "Even with the blood deliveries?"

"Oh, this was ages ago, long before I lived here. The forties, maybe?" he said breezily, mentioning the bygone decade he had lived through with such a lack of fanfare that it almost seemed like he was discussing something that had happened last week.

Carsen found herself thinking about the nearly 200 years Keaton had spent alive, or whatever iteration of life this was. How many places had he seen in that time? How many people had he befriended, fallen in love with? How many of those people must be dead now?

An understanding of the loneliness he carried between his eyebrows came to Carsen in a flash, and she felt her heart twist in compassion. What must it be like to lose everyone, again and again?

"I had started to lose the taste for human blood, or at least my appetite for all that went with it, and was looking for alternatives. Lived by a forest a lot like this one at the time. There were a lot more forests back then. Fiona would have loved it. We were just out of the Dust Bowl and trying to be kinder to the land so it would never happen again. There was this one fellow, Louis Bromfield, a bigshot writer who ended up doing environmental preservation work, or the early version of it. He had the most beautiful house..." He was lost in the memory, and Carsen left him there to savor it for a second.

"Anyways. The first time happened after I had gone a week and a half without blood. I was so hungry by then I could

205

barely stand it. I had this terrible habit of just trying to wait out the thirst, see if I could beat it, and simply live on nothing. Obviously, I never could. And by then, I'd be so weak, so panicked, so desperate that I'd take anything I could get my hands on, and far more of it than I actually needed, feeling like I would never be able to get enough. And the cycle would begin again, with me feeling only worse for having tried and then failing so spectacularly."

He fell quiet for a moment, apparently lost in his own guilty reverie. He shook his head sadly before continuing.

"I was in New York then, upstate. I was pacing the woods like a madman. It was always so frustrating that I couldn't think my way out of the hunger. I was just about to break when I saw Atticus."

Carsen turned to face him fully, surprised. This wasn't where she had expected the story to go.

"Was it Buffalo? Or Rochester? Syracuse, maybe. I'm not entirely sure. We were all over the state during that time," Keaton mused aloud.

"I had known he lived there, of course, but not known he was like me. He kept to himself, mostly. The town doctor, but very standoffish and not a little strange. His accent was much stronger back then, much more of a brogue, and all the ladies in town found him so charming. Especially since he would cure their children for free. This was fresh off the Depression, and people were still struggling. I heard whispers from the townsfolk about him being some sort of prince, and that was why he was so rich that he could afford to work for free. To be honest, I hadn't paid him much attention. I didn't pay anyone much attention, really. I was still drinking from people, you see. I couldn't bear the thought that I might drink from someone I knew, who knew me, maybe even liked me.

"You drank from me, though," Carsen interrupted. Immediately, she was furious with herself. Keaton was so seldom open with anyone. Indeed, he seemed to have almost forgotten she was there. She doubted she'd have heard much of this otherwise. She could've saved her question for later.

Keaton didn't seem to mind, though. "I did. Why does that matter?" He didn't say it cruelly or sharply, just curious.

"Well, you drank from me, and I'm here to tell the tale. Why didn't you strike up an arrangement with someone? Surely you had a friend, someone who would want to help you." She nervously shoved her glasses up her nose, worried she had overstepped.

"I didn't have any friends because I didn't want to drink from anyone. By then, the very action of feeding was so poisonous in my mind that I would never have subjected anyone to it. Besides, I had never thought about the fact that I could stop when I had enough. The thought honestly never occurred to me. And it would never have occurred to anyone else, either. Only you would think of something like that, Carsen. Only you would give yourself up that willingly, with no strings attached." He gazed at her with something too close to admiration for her to be comfortable with it. She looked away.

"Sorry, I interrupted. What about you and Atticus and the deer?"

He seemed to know why she was changing the subject but obliged her anyway. "It seemed like he had come out of nowhere, just phased into existence right next to me. Looking back, I think I was so out of my mind with thirst that God himself could have sat down next to me and tried to strike up a conversation, and I would never have noticed."

"He didn't try to speak to me. He knew I was too far gone for conversation. He just stood there, looking me in the eyes, and then was gone. At first, I thought I had dreamed him. But then he was back, and he was carrying a deer over his shoulder. It was still alive. I could still hear the blood pumping through its veins, smell its fear. I looked at him like he'd lost his mind, but he slung the thing down to the ground and simply said 'Drink.' So I did." His eyes were almost glazed over, his mind totally in the memory.

"I drank the whole thing in this haze of confusion and starvation, and when I had finished, I could think clearly again. At first, I thought it felt better than human blood. I felt so strong, so steady. Then I realized I could taste its fear on my tongue. I stood there, letting it roll over me, the feeling of dying. It had never happened to me before. I'd read about other vampires feeling the emotions of their victims in the blood, but I thought it was just some story. I still don't know why it only started then. Maybe because I was consuming with more consciousness than before, more empathy. Up until then, it had just been about the hunt. I had nearly enjoyed the whole process. Then I served in World War I - I was mostly just interested. It was a different type of killing. I had never killed during the Civil War, just doing my abolition work and running safe houses and campaigning." Carsen was silent and totally still, enrapt. She had never heard Keaton talk about his past like this before.

"This kind of death felt like more, even than drinking their blood. I was killing them because they were there because it was what I was told to do. A loss of life with absolutely no purpose. I came back home, and all I could think was that I could never do this to a human again. The thought of tasting a human's last breath was too much for me to bear. As to the deer Atticus had brought me, I threw up its blood in the grass then and there. I'd never thrown up as a vampire before; I thought it was one of those things I just couldn't do anymore. Atticus was kind, didn't judge me, simply went and got another deer. He snapped its neck quickly, so it didn't know what was coming, and I drank it in its entirety without a break."

The deer were long gone now, and Carsen and Keaton were stood in the frozen half light, the sun starting to rise and throwing oranges and purples across the open sky.

"Why didn't you ask Frankie? To come see the deer?" Carsen

209

asked, ducking her head in thanks as she made her way through the door he was holding open.

Keaton laughed. "If anyone wakes that girl up before eight in the morning, they'll lose a head. And I'm pretty connected to mine."

Carsen wondered if that was the real reason. Keaton had never, ever spoken so openly to her, never shared his vulnerable side. Things between them were evolving, but to what?

"Well, I'm glad you asked me," she said as she planted a kiss on his mouth. She spun on one heel and headed back toward her bedroom, not needing to look back to know that his eyes were following her.

22

Coastline

Time marched forward, an indelible force that she was dreading more and more by the day. No matter how tightly she held her fingers together, the sands of time moved through them, moving her farther and farther from them. Soon the cherry blossoms were blooming, and they woke every morning to birds singing and pollen thick in the air.

May was there in no time at all, and she would have missed Beltane if she hadn't already planned a lesson for it. It was utterly unlike her, and she put it down to the exhaustion of having two rambunctious children ramming around the house all the time. Certainly nothing to do with the two sets of eyes that followed her everywhere she went.

"Do we have a giant pole laying around anywhere, by chance?" she asked breezily at breakfast the next morning, through a mouthful of oatmeal.

Atticus raised an eyebrow at her. "Not that I can think of. Maybe try the woods?"

So into the woods she went, hair sticking to the back of her neck, bugs nibbling at her ankles. She found a fallen branch close to the railroad tracks that was just barely long enough to suit her purposes. She found Maddie there too, standing alone in the forest's shade. The child was staring out across the tracks at nothing, eyes slightly dazed. Carsen felt her brow furrow as she forged her way closer to the little girl, shoving through the high grass.

"Maddie? What's wrong? Are you okay? Why are you out here by yourself?" She could hear the stream of questions coming out of her, and was reminded of Frankie, that very first day. She shook the thought away and refocused.

Maddie stared at her, and there was something empty in her eyes that made Carsen's stomach drop out of her. Just as quickly as it had come, it was gone.

"Don't worry, Carsen. Fiona and I were playing hide and seek. She's not out here though. I think I went the wrong way."

Without another word, Maddie turned and started towards the house. Carsen watched her go, feeling distinctly that something was off but not sure what it was or how to figure it out. Shaking her head and filing it away for another time, she focused her energy on levitating the sizeable fallen tree branch back to the house. As she began her walk back, following in Maddie's footsteps, she could've sworn that she heard children laughing, a faint haunting noise that made the hair on the back of her neck stand up.

–

"Is everybody ready?" Carsen called out, twisting her ribbon between her fingers.

The pole gathering had been by far the most difficult part of the preparation process. Atticus had pulled rounds of colorful ribbon from a closet somewhere ("Fiona went through a hair ribbon phase," he explained), and Keaton had gathered flowers for decorations. Frankie had dug a not insignificant hole in the ground in all of three minutes, anchored the branch upwards with ease, and hoisted Fiona up onto her shoulders to tie the seven ribbons to the top. Carsen had encouraged Atticus to invite Zahra to the ceremony, and had been pleasantly surprised when he had actually done it. Now, all seven of them were stood around the pole, each holding their own respective ribbon.

Various affirmative noises came from around the circle, and Carsen grinned. "Okay, go!" They all moved as one, circling the pole again and again, laughing as the ribbons intertwined, snake-like, down the pole. When they got towards the end, Maddie and Fiona tumbled into one another, and sat on the grass giggling like only little girls can.

Carsen felt a warmth in her lungs, like she'd breathed in a bonfire. She, startled, recognized it as love. Love for the little girls sat getting grass stains on their nice dresses, love for this house that had become a home all of the sudden after all this time. Love for…

She clapped her hands together. "Right, good job everybody! Now, if you'd like to stay for the lesson, you're welcome to. If not though…" She gestured toward the picnic table Atticus had set up on the wrap-around porch. "Frankie makes a killer lemonade."

As the adults made their way to the refreshments she was left with the enraptured eyes of Maddie and Fiona.

Carsen tried not to revel in their attention too much, but it was hard not to. It was more and more difficult to get the two of them in the same room without arguing these days, and Fiona was always spinning off like a pinball, distracted by this or that. They always sat still for her lessons though, and it made her chest hurt with pride each time. Even now they were starting to fidget, and she realized she was losing valuable time. Keeping the attention of both girls was like catching lightning in a bottle, and she didn't intend to waste it.

Carsen and her eager students sat around the bonfire Frankie had set ablaze with a bit too much delight in her eye a few hours ago. It had burned high for quite a while and now was settling into a comfortable crackle.

"Beltane is traditionally celebrated on May 1st, but you can observe it any time during the month of May. Very helpful when you're forgetful like I am. It's the time of year when the veil is thinnest, so those who commune with the fae tend to do it around this time. Personally, I don't involve them in my practice. They're slippery things. Can't be trusted."

"What's with the fire?" Maddie interrupted.

This was unusual for Maddie, who was usually a model student, but Carsen allowed it, as it was the perfect transition for her next topic.

"The fire symbolizes the sun gaining its strength as summer comes. Lots of people jump over bonfires during their ceremonies for good luck during the year." She gazed appraisingly over her glasses at the pair of them. "Either of you have any interest in doing that?"

They both shook their heads vehemently. Carsen smiled and returned to her lesson.

"The Maypole is generally thought to be symbolic of the seasons changing from spring into summer. To be honest, in all my reading, I've not been able to find a super clear answer on its actual purpose. I think it's fun, though. So I like to do it. Maddie, when we start getting to the end of our lessons and start to move towards making your own independent practice, we can chat about what things you want to keep and drop."

By now, the girls were getting antsy - Fiona was visibly bouncing in her seat - so Carsen decided it was best to call it a day. She congratulated the girls on their attentiveness and told Maddie they would meet again soon. As they left, she turned to look at the bonfire, thinking hard.

Suddenly, damning the aching in her hips, Carsen leaped over the fire. She landed hard, her knees on the other side, grunting with the impact. Quickly looking around to see that no one had noticed her, she shoved herself back up. She would be bruised tomorrow, but it was worth it.

Ready to enjoy the celebration now that her work was done, Carsen joined Keaton and Frankie, the latter of whom had flowers braided into her hair. "Nice look," Carsen said admiringly, running her fingers through the ends of her own hair, which was properly bird-nested by now.

Frankie beamed at her. "Thanks! Keaton did it."

If Keaton still had blood in his veins, he would've blushed bright red. As it was, he stared solemnly at his shoes with an expression more befitting a funeral. "I...could do it for you too, if you wanted."

Now, *this* was truly a surprise. Not wanting to waste the opportunity to feel Keaton's fingers in her hair, she accepted immediately.

"Let's go inside. I'd prefer not to have an audience, or the girls will be begging me to do their hair every day," Keaton said.

Frankie turned and began to walk away, murmuring under her breath, "As though he wouldn't love that."

–

They sat cross-legged on Carsen's bed, Keaton gently brushing her hair out over her shoulders and Frankie rubbing circles on the top of her hand.

"When did you learn to do this?" she asked, leaning into Keaton's touch as much as she could without making it obvious, embarrassed by her neediness.

"You pick up things over the years when you've been around as long as I have." His voice was low, soothing.

When he finished, Frankie gazed at her like she'd captured the moon in a net and brought it to Earth just for her. "Could I see you two in the bedroom, please?"

-

It was a heady feeling, having the two of them holding her down, Frankie grasping at her wrists, and Keaton with a gentle but firm grip on her ankles. She felt imminently breakable, a strange contrast with the knowledge that if anything did break her, the perpetrator would have hell to pay from these two.

"Do you want this?" Keaton asked, pushing up her dress. He sounded breathless, out of control in a way that she'd never seen him be. It looked good on him.

"Yes," she breathed. And they went to work.

They were each the opposite of what she had expected, always

217

so different from her anticipations. Keaton's touch was feather-light, almost worshipful, nearly reverent. He treated her like a china doll and touched her like a strong breeze would shatter her. It was completely antithetical to the firm and occasionally harsh man that she knew. Frankie, on the other hand, was relentless, leaving her panting and shaking and spent.

Frankie leaned in very close to her and whispered into her ear. "You can't hide anything from us, baby. We can hear your little hummingbird heart from a mile away."

-

"When are we going to talk about this? Like, properly talk about it." Frankie said this from her spot next to her, lying on her stomach, gazing up at Carsen like she was a particularly beautiful sunset. Keaton was on her other side, looking drowsy and contented. Carsen's heart hurt with how much she loved them, how much she wanted this to be forever.

"What's there to talk about? I thought we'd already sorted this. You're both mine, and that's all there is to it." Keaton's voice was surprisingly steady.

"But just this way? Are we yours outside these walls, too? What will Atticus say?" Frankie asked.

Carsen suddenly felt a rush of frustration in her lungs. "Who cares what he says? I want you both, properly."

Keaton smirked at this, and he danced his fingertips across

218

her skin. "You both know I've been around a while. This is hardly the strangest thing I've ever been involved in." Keaton's voice was teasing, and he beamed at the both of them. Carsen sat quietly for a moment before turning to Frances. "What about you?"

"My answer is yes," Frankie said, flipping over to her back. She was smiling a bit, but she still had an uncharacteristic furrow in her brow, and Carsen reached to smooth it out.

"What is it that you're worried about?" Carsen whispered into her hair, lips ghosting along her neck.

"You'll leave. That's why you're so hesitant." Frankie replied, eyes sad.

Carsen went stock still. She was right, and Carsen had no response for it.

It was Keaton who delivered the response in the end. "Things that are temporary are still just as beautiful. I know that better than anybody."

He sighed contentedly. "My girls." He turned his head to press a kiss to Carsen's forehead.

Frankie was already snoring. Carsen giggled softly so as not to wake her and then wiggled her way further into their shared blanket. She felt incredibly safe between her two monsters.

"It feels like we're in a dream,[19]" she whispered.

Keaton said nothing, merely smiling and kissing her forehead.

The room was dark, the window just the slightest bit pushed up so that the steady pounding rain could tuck them in.

23

Seven

"Would you do me too?" Frankie asked, looking appraisingly down at where Carsen sat on her bedroom floor, sticking and poking protective runes into her shin.

"Sure. Come on down," she answered, patting the floor next to her with the hand not holding a needle.

"Do you want one, Keaton?" she added, sensing his quiet presence in the doorframe. "It looks cool *and* serves a purpose. Pretty awesome, right?"

"Yes, very cool," he said, the last word sounding strange on his ancient tongue. "But my venom will burn the ink out of my skin. It won't stay. I've tried before. I'll sit and watch, though."

Carsen hummed agreement and heard her bed creak as Keaton curled up on the bed like a cat, peering over the side to observe them. She returned to her work, endlessly poking holes into her skin.

"What does it mean?" Frankie asked, craning to get a better look at the strange interwoven circle.

"It's a Celtic shield knot," Carsen answered, not looking up. "Protective symbol. It's supposed to help with illness and strengthen you in battle." She didn't say that although she hoped it would work for the former, she was really counting on it working its magick to do the latter. Something was coming. She wasn't sure what, but she wanted to be prepared. She did the last few lines and appraised her work. Satisfied, she turned to Frankie.

"Do you want the same one or something different?"

"Something different, I think. Something you pick for me."

Carsen gazed at her for a moment, assessing. She looked into her amber eyes and searched for something wanting. A lightbulb popped on.

"Do you trust me?" she asked suddenly.

"Duh." Frankie answered, looking almost offended by the question.

"Enough to let me do this without looking at what I'm doing first?"

In answer, Frankie stuck her legs out, laid back, and shut her

222

eyes.

Smiling, Carsen started to ink the design into Frankie's leg. They sat in companionable silence as Carsen poked hundreds of holes into Frankie's skin. Blood bubbled up from her work, and she stopped to wipe it clean.

"Does it not bother you?" Carsen asked Keaton, looking up from her work curiously. "She's bleeding."

"Sadly, I only lust for the blood of mortals. Especially ones who are five feet tall and annoying," Keaton said seriously. Then he leaned down and kissed her neck. Carsen flushed, pleased with herself. "I especially like the ones who blush." His mock tone of sincerity made Frances roll over and laugh.

Looking like the cat who got the cream, Keaton flopped back onto the bed and onto his stomach dramatically, landing face-first on her pillows and breathing deeply. He groaned and then yanked a sweater out from under one of them.

"Hey! I've been looking for this! You scoundrel!"

Carsen tried to look abashed but couldn't quite manage it. "Sorry. I got cold."

Actually, she hadn't been cold. She had stolen something of Frankie's too - a T-shirt she never wore. She was a crow hoarding shiny things, gathering memories of memories.

Finished, she sat back, holding her back gingerly. She would need to make some willow bark tea after this.

"It's a triskele. Another Celtic symbol." She had added some leaves and berries around it, just for a little flare. It was quite cute, and Carsen preened at her handiwork.

Frankie leaned forward to investigate. "What does it mean?"

"That the most important things in life come in threes."

–

They had finally convinced Atticus to stop hiding Zahra in town, and he had finally allowed Frankie to invite her to dinner. Frankie had been beyond delighted. She had spent all week baking and looking up recipes until the kitchen looked like they were preparing for an army to come to dinner rather than one extra person.

Zahra arrived ten minutes early in her tank of a jeep to much fanfare. The girls were enamored with her and her feline beauty and her funny riddles. It was, it turned out, quite fun to have a sphinx at your dinner party.

Atticus shyly kissed her cheek, looking abashed. Keaton looked pleased as punch to see him uncomfortable, and Carsen privately wondered how much teasing he himself had endured about her and Frankie from Atticus.

After eating more than any one person ever should, the three women stood on the porch watching the girls play. Screeches of delight echoed around the wooded area as the girls ran around the yard, Maddie having summoned a windstorm to chase after Fiona.

"Don't you miss that?" Frankie asked, eyes fond.

"I certainly do. I hit my peak at seven,[20]" Carsen joked, not joking at all.

"All little girls have magick in their veins," Zahra said simply, face serious. "Some more than most." This last sentence was pointed, her gaze hanging on Maddie.

24

Invisible String / Shrike

May came in a burst of rain and unseasonable heat. The air was heavy with humidity and the scent of honeysuckle, drowning you in it the second you stepped outside. It was even hotter inside the house, though, with their lack of air conditioning and the heat being stirred up in one of the threes' bedrooms every night.

"You wanna bite me so bad," Carsen teased.

His eyes flashed. "I do, huh?" Suddenly, he was there, fangs grazing against her bare neck. "Do you want to push me?"

She swallowed, and he felt the movement in his stomach. "I really, really do."

"I wanted you the minute you walked in the door," he murmured, reverently stroking her skin. Keaton looked wild - eyes feral, hair a mess. She liked him this way.

"You were so quiet when I got here. So standoffish," she gasped into him.

Keaton was breathless. She didn't think that vampires could get breathless. "Well, I'm singing like a bird about it now,[21] aren't I?"

—

Frankie had made a gigantic cake for Keaton's birthday, so big that Carsen wasn't entirely sure how she had fit it into the oven. When Keaton had chided her for the extravagance, she hadn't even pretended to be abashed.

"You need one big enough for all your candles!" she insisted.

Keaton rolled his eyes fondly. "Are you really expecting to fit all 175 candles onto that cake?"

She was, and she somehow managed it. It was a terrible fire hazard, the cake nearly aflame with the amount of candles lit on top of it, and Carsen had laughed so hard she nearly wheezed with it.

Frankie had installed a porch swing (Keaton and Carsen had observed, handing her the necessary screwdrivers and holding onto nails), and that night, as the dark descended and the fireflies began to do their incandescent dance, they sat together on the cozy, swaying bench..

"Do you think we were meant for each other?" Frankie asked.

Carsen cocked her head, but Keaton answered immediately.

"Yes. I felt pulled along all these years. Like there was some invisible string[22] stuck in my chest, tugging me to a target I couldn't quite see. Now, I know where I was going. I was coming for you two.

25

Witches

When she came down to the kitchen the next morning, she found her two monsters bouncing up and down on their heels, chattering quietly. When they turned to her, their eyes were bright, and Carsen felt a swooping in her stomach. It was still a surprise to her to feel this amount of joy merely at the sight of someone. Let alone two someones.

"What are you two up to?" she asked, eyebrows raised.

"We have a surprise for you!" Frankie was absolutely jovial.

"Close your eyes." Keaton stepped forward and then stood behind her, holding her and covering her face with his two large hands.

Carsen giggled and reached her hands up to Keaton's, partly to steady herself but mostly to hold his hands.

She allowed him to guide her, practically on top of his shoes, being walked from room to room like a child. She could hear Frankie's laughing, a joyful sound that made her stomach bubble. Suddenly, they were at the front door - she could feel the morning chill just managing to skate across her nose.

"I'm not wearing shoes!" she said quickly, not wanting her socks soaked with dew. Almost instantly, Keaton's strong arms were around her, and she had been lifted in the air, held tight against his chest.

"Keep your eyes closed, missy," he murmured, a low thing that rumbled against her skin. She could feel where the sound left his chest, and it made her feel like a live wire.

"Okay," she whispered, mouth dry.

They moved quickly across the yard, her feeling his every steady step, hearing Frankie saying things like "I can't wait for you to see it!" and "Watch out for that tree root, Keaton, don't jostle her."

She didn't even care where they were going. She wanted to stay in his arms like this forever, hear Frankie's voice as a soundtrack for the rest of her life. But they arrived at their destination nonetheless, and he was calmly murmuring in her ear, "I'm putting you down now, alright? Keep those eyes closed."

Her feet were being set down on a wooden floor - she could feel the plats between her toes. She could hear Keaton

230

moving around and then pull some sort of curtain back. He returned to them, and she could feel them on either side of her, Frankie's heat and Keaton's lukewarm.

"Okay, you can open your eyes!" Frankie sounded like she could burst.

Carsen opened her eyes and gasped.

They were in some sort of garden shed, but it was covered in greenery. Her drying herbs had been moved from the kitchen, and some of her books were on a bookshelf that she recognized from the living room. But most striking of all was the back wall. One of them, likely Keaton, had painted a mural there, her name in beautiful cursive slants, with delicately detailed flowers pinwheeling off of the letters. She moved closer to the wall to examine it, breathless with the beauty of it.

"It's a place for you to work on your rituals and potions and stuff! You could dry your herbs from the rafters, and Keaton put in a little hearth for your cauldron," Frankie chattered excitedly.

"We've been taking turns getting it ready for you in the evening." Keaton's voice was low and pleased.

It was the nicest thing anybody had ever done for her.

Turning around, eyes shining, she whispered, "thank you," unable to help the reverence in her tone.

231

Keaton smiled shyly. Frankie beamed. Carsen was so terribly happy that her lungs ached.

"We were thinking that this winter, you could try and grow some herbs inside. I know you said that the potions work better with fresh materials." Frankie was running her finger along the solid wooden table sat in the middle of the room. Keaton was examining his handiwork on the mural, nose nearly touching the wall.

Her stomach dropped at the thought of what she was going to have to say to them.

She plowed forward. "But...I thought you knew. I thought Atticus had told you... At the end of the summer, I'm gone. I'm only here on a one-year contract."

Their faces fell in tandem, but Frankie's quickly picked back up again.

"Well, you don't need a contract to stay here! We don't have a contract. We just live here. You can live here, with us. Like a family."

Carsen thought she might throw up. "But...I have to go home, Franks. I have to take over the family apothecary and help my mom."

Frankie looked as though she'd been punched. Keaton's face had become a pale mask, eyes shuttered.

"I thought this was your home?" Frankie protested, sounding

232

shattered.

Carsen felt her heart split in two. "It is! It is, I-" but it was too late. Frankie backed up, looking strained. She let out a little groan, seemingly against her will, and then doubled over in pain.

"Franks?" Carsen asked, stepping towards her, but Keaton pulled her back, hands gentle even as his jaw was so tight it looked as though it might snap.

She was changing before her very eyes, her nose stretching out into a snout and black nails shooting from her fingers. Keaton shoved Carsen behind him, back taut with tension. Holding her arm with a vicelike grip that was utterly unlike him, he moved around the room, his other hand up in a sign of surrender, to the door. He opened it and pulled Carsen outside.

"We'll give her some privacy," Keaton said stonily, not looking at her.

"I didn't mean to-"

"I know."

He didn't sound like himself, but Carsen didn't have time to be miserable about it because Frankie, fully a wolf, was jumping through the air, pushing off from her hind legs and launching through the doorway. For a moment, she hung there, weightless. It was the most spectacular thing Carsen had ever seen.

She came down to the earth soundlessly, paws giant. Her large amber eyes met Carsen's, and the sadness in them made Carsen want to throw herself into the ocean. She moved towards the wolf, ignoring Keaton's protestations. The wolf watched her, impassive.

Carsen reached out both arms and hugged her around her giant neck. She couldn't bear to look at her and her moonlit eyes.[23]

"Please don't be mad at me," she whispered into her soft fur.

Frankie huffed and rested her heavy jaw in Carsen's small hand. She felt like Atlas.

Without warning, Frankie lifted her head from her and bolted away. Carsen started after her, but Keaton blocked her path.

"Let her go. She needs some time."

Carsen's eyes were saucers. She didn't know how this could possibly have all gone so poorly so quickly.

"Keaton, I-"

"I need some time too," he interrupted, refusing to look at her. He turned and walked in the opposite direction.

Carsen sat down in the grass, still wearing her pajamas, and wept.

26

Where's My Love

Frankie didn't change back for two full days. Carsen watched the wolf pace the perimeter of the house, feeling nauseous and lonely. Keaton said nothing to anyone, which made her feel worse. Atticus had kindly brought tea to her when she had returned to her room in tears after their fight, but he had said nothing. She knew he knew everything, knew that the intimate details of their conversation had probably made the rounds by now. The girls had been skittish around her ever since, and she felt badly. She really had assumed that everybody knew, had figured that Atticus would have explained the parameters of their agreement. In retrospect, she had been cowardly and hoped that he had done the hard work for her. She should've known he would never have said anything.

She laid in bed the second evening having skipped dinner to hide in her room, too ashamed to face anyone. There was a tiny knock on the door, and Carsen prepared herself for a dressing down.

A tiny blonde head popped in through the doorway.

Fiona walked right up to the side of her bed where Carsen was laying, drowning in self pity, and patted her hand. "I like you. I hope you stay."

To receive a compliment from a child is somehow more powerful than those from adults. Children are so discerning, and so capable of a brutal honesty that verges on cruelty. It makes their kindness more genuine.

Carsen swallowed a sob and clasped the child's tiny hand in hers. "Thank you, Fiona. That means a lot to me."

The little girl left the room, and she could hear Keaton outside her door, gathering Fiona and taking her to brush her teeth before bed. She ached with the knowledge that he wouldn't be in to see her tonight, and maybe not even the night after that.

Carsen crawled to the window next to her bed, struggling to navigate over the tossed blankets. She opened it the slightest bit, barely enough to feel a breeze, and pressed her lips to the opening.

"Just come home[24]," she whispered into the darkness. She knew yelling would be unnecessary. Frankie could hear her just as well as if they were right next to each other. "Just come home. I'll never ask anything more of you or make you suffer ever again."

The woods remained silent.

–

When she woke up at half past three that morning, Carsen looked through her window and barely stifled a scream.

Two golden glowing eyes were staring steadily at her through the dark.

She struggled to her feet as fast as she could, not even pausing to throw on shoes before she ran outside to meet the wolf.

Carsen stuttered to a stop, standing stock still in her socked feet in front of the largest animal she had ever seen. Frankie.

She was beautiful, even in this monstrous form she had so often bemoaned. The hair was the same dark brown, the eyes the same lovely amber. It was Frankie, but more. Frankie, with no boundaries apparently, as this Frankie moved closer and began to smell Carsen thoroughly. She sniffed at her face and then licked the tears away.

Carsen gave a wet laugh. "I'm so sorry, baby. I am so sorry."

She would've said more, but a terrible sound came from behind her. She turned around to look. Another wolf, a real wolf, stood behind them, hackles up, growling ferociously. She heard a low snarl and knew that Frankie was lowering herself into a protective stance.

Wolf Frankie (she kept catching herself differentiating in her head, she still wasn't totally sure where the animal stopped, and her Frankie started) lowered her head and ran, catching the thing square in the chest with a head butt and sending it spinning over its own head.

The air left her lungs almost in tandem with Frankie ramming the wolf. "Frankie!" Her voice was choked, eyes almost impossibly wide. The wolf tumbled, whining as it hit the ground. It skittered itself upright and ran deeper into the woods. Frankie turned her eyes on Carsen.

"Baby, baby, I'm sorry. I'm sorry." Carsen whispered, tears pouring down her cheeks. Frankie's tongue reached out and licked her ear. She giggled despite herself.

There was a terrible twisting, and Frankie was Frankie again, without a stitch of clothing on. The weather was nice enough that Carsen didn't worry about her freezing or being uncomfortable; just drank in the sight.

"I know. I know you're sorry. I was just...a little heartbroken, is all."

Carsen winced. The depth of what she had done was starting to crash over her.

When she went to knock on Keaton's door, she found the door ajar and him practicing his cello furiously. When he looked up to find her in the doorway, his eyes widened.

"I'm sorry," they said simultaneously.

239

Carsen blinked. "I'm sorry-" she tried again, but Keaton interrupted her with the same phrase. They both laughed a little, embarrassed at how ridiculous they sounded.

"I shouldn't have acted the way I did," Keaton said. "I was upset that Frankie was upset, and I took it out on you. It's not your fault."

"I should've been more clear," Carsen answered his apology with one of her own. "I was scared, and I thought I'd let Atticus do the hard work for me. Shows what I know."

Keaton gave her a half smile. She sensed him holding something back but allowed him to keep his secrets while he could. She knew now how hard it was to lose hold of things.

27

Heat Waves - Stripped Back

O ne morning, Keaton didn't come to breakfast.
Atticus didn't say anything, but he was clearly
worried. He vacated the kitchen earlier than
normal, taking the girls outside. It went unsaid that he
was allowing Carsen and Frankie to conference about the
situation.

"You should go talk to him. He's in the bathroom," Frankie
said. Atticus had barely left the room. She'd clearly been dying
to tell her this.

"How do you know? What's wrong with him? Why just me?"
A torrent of questions left her in one rush of breath.

"He had a nightmare last night. I already checked on him, I
could hear him since our rooms are right next to each other."

Carsen swept along towards the bathroom, stomach turning.
She knocked gently on the closed door and opened the door

to the quietest "come in" that she'd ever heard.

Keaton was on the floor, crying. Carsen knelt next to him, reaching out to hold him. He lurched away, and she stopped short, trying to hide her hurt.

"What's wrong? What happened?" she asked.

"You need something I could never give.[25] Someone warm. Someone human." He was crying. She'd never seen him cry. The redness in his eyes made the blue stronger somehow, and she reached out a hand to touch his.

"I don't want human. I want you."

"What if I hurt you? I couldn't live with that, and I'm doomed to live forever, Carsen. I will bear the burden of my mistakes for all eternity."

"Why are you thinking these things?"

"I had a bad dream," he answered. "I don't want to be alone.[26]" Keaton's raw voice shattered Carsen - she felt the fissure starting in her heart and moving all the way through to her toes.

Keaton went on. "But I don't know if it's fair to you to continue this, to let you get close to me when there are so many things wrong with this picture."

"I like this picture. Let me pick who I get close to. This isn't the 20th century anymore. Women make their own decisions."

This seemed to rouse him from the fit of emotion, and the storm on his face cleared a bit. "You're right. Of course, you're right."

She smiled and hugged him, not believing a word he said.

—

Later, Carsen found Maddie sitting near the edge of the woods, cross-legged and contemplative.

She plopped down next to her as gracefully as she could, using her cane to help balance. "What's up?"

Maddie, with a voice that sounded older than the hills, said, "I think I'm more of a grown-up than a kid."

Carsen gazed at her, irrevocably reminded of a day a decade prior when she'd said the same very thing, and laughed aloud.

"Why are you laughing?" Maddie demanded, expression already shuttering.

Remembering how agonizing it is to be eleven and think that everyone is in on a joke that you know nothing about, Carsen immediately schooled her face into a solemn one. "I just think you and I are very similar."

Maddie brightened. "You think so?"

243

Warmed by the idea that someone would think that a good thing, Carsen nodded. "Absolutely."

–

Carsen should've known it would end badly the minute that Atticus came into the living room wielding a syringe. It was a gigantic needle, visible in the way that her preferred butterfly needles were never.

Keaton was on his feet in seconds, positioning his body in front of hers. Frankie did the same thing, fists clenched.

"Are you sure this time?" Keaton demanded of Atticus.

"This isn't an exact science. It's one big experiment, and she knows that. It's what she signed up for. Carsen, are you ready?"

She lifted her chin and extended her arm, swallowing hard. "Yes."

Keaton and Frankie each backed up slightly, creating a kind of gauntlet for Atticus to traverse. Atticus made his way purposely through the challenge and brushed against Keaton, perhaps intentionally and perhaps not. Keaton's fangs were out in a flash. Carsen whispered his name, and he begrudgingly put them away.

"Are you ready?" Atticus asked again, seeming unsure as he knelt to inject the medication.

She forced her shoulders down from around her ears. "Let's do it."

The moment the needle entered her skin, Carsen was on fire. She could feel what had to be some sort of toxin sprinting through her veins, setting each part of her that it touched aflame. Her lungs burned, her toes singed, everything an agonizing heat. Her hands reached wildly out for Frankie and Keaton and found them waiting for her.

She screamed.

"Carsen, stop! You're scaring the girls," Atticus said, hands hovering above her body, clearly wanting to help but not sure how.

Keaton whirled around to face Atticus, and for the first time, Carsen was truly scared of him.

"Good! They should be scared. They should see exactly what you're capable of." He returned his gaze to Carsen, eyes wild with concern. "Say something, sweetheart."

The pain was fading, and her vice grip on her monsters was loosening. "It's okay. I'm okay. It's passing." She sighed as the remainder of the burn left her.

"Any change?" Atticus asked pointedly not looking at Keaton.

She assessed her joints, clicking them in and out.

"Still hurts," she reported. "No change."

28

The Archer

Carsen was having more and more nightmares - it was starting to be nearly every night. They were always the same, and they always sparkled in a way that let her know there was something at least a little real about them.

The nightmares started with her walking in the woods alone, leaning on her cane more than usual. She would come into an unfamiliar clearing, out of breath, to find some Thing waiting for her.

It was human-shaped, while anything but. Its skin was tree bark, moss growing up one side of the face and into the eye. a thorny vine emerged from the being's stomach and then curled around it, wrapping up and up until it protruded through the eye not covered in moss. Eyes wide, teeth bared in some semblance of a smile, it would speak to her.

"I have an offering."

Carsen knew every time that this was a trap. "What's the price?" she would ask.

"Nothing of import."

"There's always a price," Carsen would whisper, more repeating something that she'd been told a thousand times rather than adding anything meaningful to the conversation.

Usually, she would wake up in a cold sweat and not sleep a wink the rest of the night. That night, the dream went further.

The creature laughed, high and wild. "It'll be worth your while. Don't you hate the way they look at you? They know you're weak. They hear you cry at night. You don't even try to hide the pain on your face! You're an embarrassment to them. You could make all that go away."

The Thing abruptly became an amalgam of Frankie and Keaton, switching between their two forms so quickly she felt sick to her stomach, though that could've been from the shame burning a pit in her intestines.

Carsen had spent her entire life trying to force every atom of her being to appear strong. She had hidden in bathrooms to vomit and then left smiling seconds later, forgone pain medication because getting it would mean admitting something she couldn't say aloud. She learned to cry quietly, in a way that left no tear tracks, no splotches on her cheeks, because anything else would be an embarrassment. She had thought she had hidden the ugly, vulnerable piece of herself away where no one could find it.

They see right through me[27], she thought.

"Can you see right through me?[28]" she asked Frankie-Keaton, nails cutting bloody half moons into the palms of her hands.

The Thing was gone and had left a strange, wrong version of Carsen herself in its place. Her own voice echoed back to her, sounding half there.

"I see right through me,[29]" Halfway-Carsen confirmed.

She should've been more afraid. This her was pale and blotchy, eyes wide, ugly and fearful. Her mouth was half open, perpetually on the verge of saying something and then thinking better of it. It didn't look anything like her, and it looked exactly like her. This was the Carsen that she'd stared in the eyes in every mirror she'd ever crossed paths with.

She woke up before she could respond to the Thing's offer.

She would have said yes.

IV

Summer

29

Boreas

C arsen started her Monday morning, laying prone on the cold linoleum[30] floor, using the ground as an ice pack, in staggering pain. As per.

That was the thing about the pain. It would be a low-level buzz throughout her being for days at a time, waxing and waning but always just on this side of manageable. Then something would happen - standing too long, lifting something the slightest bit too heavy, missing just that little bit too much sleep. It would all come crashing down; her elegant charade cracked down the center, all of her work undone in an instant.

There was the softest of knocks at the door, and then Frankie let herself in.

"Why didn't you say something?" The other woman asked, sinking to the floor.

"If I said something every time I was in pain, I'd never stop talking about it. It would be so awfully boring for everybody else and for me." She was going for levity, but it came out bitter, and she hated herself for it.

Frankie lifted her up, cradling her in her arms as she sank back to the ground, protecting her from the cold that was now sinking into her joints. She encompassed her, a human heating pad. Carsen felt her muscles start to unclench and cried with the relief of it. She reached up with a shaking hand and angrily wiped a tear away.

"Gentle, baby." Frankie delicately pulled Carsen's hand from where it was attacking her eye and wiped the tear with her thumb.

"I can't take the pain away. I wish I could, but I can't. I can be a bit of warmth for you,[31] though. I hope that can be enough."

Carsen sighed, sinking into her touch. "It's more than enough. It's all I've ever wanted." She felt herself start to drift off to sleep. Frankie kept rubbing her thumb into the palm of Carsen's hand. It was soothing enough to take her the rest of the way.

–

That night, it wasn't the Thing in her dreams, but Winnifred Cromwell, the drowned drag herself. She stood in darkness - not in a room, not anywhere, merely surrounded by blackness. The ghost stood, silhouetted in her own light. Her white bonnet was a beacon, her mouth a scared straight line.

"Your trouble is here," she whispered, more quietly than Carsen had ever heard her.

Who knew ghosts could be frightened?

-

"I'm going to be going away soon," Maddie announced at the dinner table that evening.

Atticus stopped with a forkful of mac and cheese halfway to his mouth. "And what, pray tell, does that mean, young lady?"

"I talked to the faeries down by the railroad. They're going to help me not be a werewolf anymore."

Keaton choked on his food. Nobody moved to help him. Frankie looked more hurt than she'd ever seen a person look before. Atticus had gone stock still. It felt a bit like time had stopped, and the only indicator that life was continuing was the sound of Keaton's sputtering. He eventually reined it in enough to choke out the question on all of their tongues.

"What?"

"They said that they were coming to get me on June 21st. So. That's next week, right? Will you help me pack, Frankie? I don't know what I'm supposed to bring."

"Next Wednesday," Carsen murmured, feeling a little dizzy.

"When did you have time to meet them? Much less make a deal with them?" Keaton demanded, still panting a bit from his choking session. Frankie and Atticus were still as stone, utterly silent waiting for her response.

"That night, I ran away. Last winter. They found me, and they said I could be normal if I did something for them."

Frankie's left eye started to twitch. "What *something?*"

"I just have to go live with them for a while, and then I can come back. And I'll be able to go to school in town, and I'll never have to change and get hurt. This is good news. Why do you all look so upset?" She seemed genuinely confused by the looks on the adults' faces, and it only emphasized that much more how very young she was, despite her tween bravado.

"Why did you wait to tell us?" Carsen broke out, unable to hold her tongue any longer.

"You said you spoke with them back in the winter. Why would you wait until summer to go see them?"

All of her visions were suddenly making sense, but this didn't. Why hadn't Maddie been whisked away immediately?

"I didn't want to miss Fiona's birthday," she answered simply. Carsen blinked.

"Fiona's birthday is still three weeks away," Frankie said. She looked as though she'd been stabbed. Carsen was tempted to look for a physical wound.

"They said that if I came now, the wolf would be gone by then. And I can feel things getting closer to me, so I agreed."

Carsen closed her eyes, trying to center herself.

The trouble was here.

30

August (Acoustic)

The next morning, Maddie wouldn't wake up. They had all tried, even Fiona.

At half past ten, she suddenly stood from the bed, eyes still closed, and took a single step. An hour later, another step.

They met in the kitchen, asking Fiona to play in the living room. Carsen knew Fiona was sitting at the shut door, ear pressed to the door, desperate for any sort of information, and she was sure the rest of the grown-ups knew it as well. They allowed it.

"Atticus, Keaton, can't you read her mind or something? Figure out what's happening?" Frankie demanded, hair half in and half out of her braids from where she'd been pulling at it.

"I don't need to read her mind to know what's happening," Keaton said, sounding deadened. "It's the faeries. They've put a trance on her. My guess is they've got her doing a step every hour. Just the sort of sick thing they'd do. She'll go till she gets to them, to the railroad. They'll make her cross it of her own volition, and then they'll take her. We'll never see her again."

Carsen narrowed her eyes at Keaton. A thousand little details were flying together all at once. She understood suddenly.

"They're the reason you can't go into town, aren't they?" she asked, tilting her head.

Keaton looked up, startled. "How did you..."

"I'm not an idiot, Keaton. You haven't left this house since I got here, and I know damn sure it's not of your own volition."

He gritted his teeth. "About ten years ago, I tried to make a deal. I wanted to not be...*this* anymore. They agreed, but I realized at the last moment what they would take from me. I would've been their slave, their immortal errand boy. I came to Atticus, who was living out here past the iron railroad. I asked him to protect me. They can't cross the railroad, you know. The iron, it hurts them to be near it. So now I live here. As long as I'm on the other side of the road, they can't touch me. If I ever go across, they'd have me in a heartbeat."

"We need to get back to the matter at hand. What are we going to do about Maddie?" Atticus asked. He looked positively ill with stress, face drawn, shadows like bruises under his eyes.

Frankie was gazing at Carsen expectantly. "It's magick versus magick. You'll be able to fix this, right?"

Frankie sounded so sure of Carsen's abilities that her heart broke. Would Frankie love her after this?

"I...I can't fix this. I'm not that powerful, and the powers I do have are pretty limited, at least in this situation. I'm useless."

Suddenly a dam that had been cracking open for years shattered into a million pieces, and Carsen heard herself make a sound that she didn't know she was capable of producing. "I'm so sorry," she whispered.

"We don't have the time,[32]" Keaton murmured, not unkindly. He turned his attention to the group. "What's the plan?"

"We might not be as powerful as them, but we're smarter," Frankie said, gathering herself.

Carsen's mind was wild, searching for a solution in every corner. Suddenly, a thought niggled at the back of her brain. She followed the path it led her down, ignoring the noise of the room. It might work.

"I have an idea," she interrupted. "And If we do this right, we might be able to break Keaton's curse as well."

31

Rises the Moon

Carsen went alone to the railroad to gather the iron, holding just a hammer. Adrenaline was pulsing through her body in a way that made her feel vaguely nauseated. When she made it to the rail line, they were waiting for her. Four of the Things from her dreams, shifting on their feet. A show of force. She kept her head down, grunting as she lowered herself to a seated position. She started to hammer.

She didn't need much- the iron was just a way to concentrate the spell. It was a good thing, too, because even though the railroad was crumbling, it was still hard work. Sweat dripped into her eyes, which helped because then she could see their pacing less. Their footsteps were loud, though, louder than they'd been in her dreams, and she had the hunch that they were doing it on purpose. It seemed that they were only increasing in volume. Finally, she had gathered enough, and laboriously, she shoved herself to her feet. She turned to go but hesitated.

She spun around.

"You will never touch my family again," she said into the open air.

There was no answer.

–

Carsen lay on her stomach in Frankie's bed, head propped up in her hands. She watched Frankie, who was pounding the iron into earrings, four small studs. She would make the iron into small circles and then set them into slightly larger circles of tourmaline to increase the protective quality. It was a steady hammering that slowly but eventually led Carsen to be visited by sleep.

–

Carsen was drowning. She cast about in the water desperately, searching for a way to the light breaking through the blue above her, but she only sank deeper. She was hot, so very hot, and she couldn't seem to get any air. There was a kind voice from the heavens, whispering in her ear to "breathe, breathe, breathe.[33]" She wanted to tell the voice that she was trying, she really was, but she was suffocating, trapped in her own skin.

"Carsen!"

Her eyes opened to find Frankie's worried face above her.

"They're ready."

–

"It's a fairly complex camouflaging spell. It will be like you don't exist to them - they will forget the promises, they will forget you both. You can never take these out, though. I had Frankie coat them with a water-repellent layer so you can even shower with them," Carsen explained, watching Keaton closely. He'd been incredibly cagey since his secret had come out, and she worried about what was going through that blond head of his. He nodded in agreement but nothing more.

"This'll be fine for you, right?"

He looked questioningly at her.

"I'm basically staking you with iron. This won't kill you, will it?"

He smiled, a small thing. She felt her chest relax a little.

"The iron thing has been greatly exaggerated."

"Alright. Good. I'm going to my room to cast the spell. Get ready to be pierced." She turned before she left the room.

"I love you, you know. We all do."

His face was tight. "I know. I love you, too."

–

She laid the jewelry down on her desk, hands shaking slightly. Although she hadn't said anything to the others, this was a bit out of her comfort range. She had never done a spell this strong before. The moonlight laid a path through her window across her floor, and she went to stand in it for a moment, feeling its light on her face. She thought about the generations of Cromwell women who had done the same thing, of Frankie and her strained relationship with the moon. Of Maddie and her fear of lost girlhood.

Carsen laid her hands on the iron and closed her eyes. She imagined Maddie and Keaton's worlds shrinking down beneath her fingers and then expanding again. "Keaton Beauregard and Maddie Hastings are no more. They are ghosts in the wind, shadows on the ground. They will not be seen, cannot be touched." She visualized Keaton's face as she had just seen it, pale, jaw working, blond hair disastrous, and saw him dissolve. She looked for Maddie where she stood in the yard, just at the entryway to the forest, and saw her vanish. Carsen smiled.

Her fingers had gone numb; the only feeling left the low electric buzz of unconfined magick. She was really too old for this sort of thing.

–

"Would you stop moving!" Carsen scolded.

For a vampire who was nearly two hundred years old, Keaton was a real baby. "That hurt way worse than you said it would!"

"Literal babies handle this better than you are right now."

"You can hold my hand if you want, sweetheart," Frankie offered.

He took it and closed his eyes. She finished the job, piercing his other ear. The minute the stud went through, his whole body relaxed. She had never noticed how tense he was. His shoulders, which she had only ever seen up around his ears, were back where they should be.

Maddie was easier, being that she was completely unconscious. She stood a few feet into the forest, just under the shade of a large oak tree. Carsen did the right ear, then the left, and the moment that the left one went in, Maddie fell to the ground.

"Maddie!" Carsen cried out, reaching for the little girl.

Frankie carried her back and put her to bed herself. Later that evening, when she woke up as if from a long nap, they all were waiting for her.

32

Achilles, Come Down

C arsen fell asleep early that night, sheer exhaustion yanking her eyelids closed without her having much of a say in the matter.

"Can you hear me?[34]" a whisper echoed, banging around in her skull. The voice was a low, silky thing, but the words were loud and painful, a clatter of sound.

"Yes," she murmured, hoping the answer would quiet the voice.

She could hear a smile, hear skin stretch to accommodate teeth. She felt sick.

"Good."

Suddenly, she stood on the edge of a cliff. The world was so green, so lush. She wanted to lay in the grass, to feel it on her skin. She knew if she went, there would be no pain, no suffering. She would be good enough for both Frankie and

Keaton.

"Come down,[35]" the voice whispered again. "End it all now. It's a pointless resistance for you.[36]"

The words were sharp on her neck and felt nothing like Keaton's fangs or Wolf Frankie's teeth. A drop of blood landed at her feet. Her blood. She let out a little gasp and stepped forward, half a footstep closer to the edge.

"You're not like them, and you know it. You've always known it from the moment you walked in the door, and yet you continue to pretend. You weren't meant to be here. You would do them a favor, to unburden them of you and your silly human frailty."

Carsen closed her eyes and lifted her foot to step over the cliff and into the forever land beneath her.

"CARSEN!"

Her body, her real body, was falling, falling, falling.

Suddenly, too suddenly, it stopped.

–

Her eyes flew open. It was bright, too bright. *Fuck.* Carsen had never believed in heaven or hell, and now she was stuck in one of the two, unsure of which.

267

"What-the-hell-was-that?" Frankie demanded, panting as though she had run a long distance very quickly.

So she was in heaven then.

"I'd quite like to know the same thing," Keaton's voice came to her from very close. Wrapped around her close. Her eyes adjusted.

She was somehow not dead. Keaton was beneath her, having absorbed her fall. His undead body looked no worse for wear, but she felt as though she'd been hit by a truck. She sat up suddenly, too suddenly, and flung a hand out to catch her as she lolled to the side.

"None of that yet," Keaton's voice was in her ear. She blinked. His arms were wrapped around her like he had been a parachute. She blinked even harder. Had he been her parachute?

"What happened?"

"You sleepwalked right off the roof; that's what happened. You would have died if Keaton hadn't jumped after you and wrapped himself around you." Frankie sounded angrier than she'd ever heard her.

Carsen leaned back fully this time, tilting her head back to rest it on Keaton's shoulder. His skin was cool against hers - she felt feverish.

"Keaton, are you alright?" It was all she could think to say.

"I'm fine. Invulnerable, remember?" He almost pouted as he said it.

"You still haven't given an answer. What happened?"

"It was that damn faerie. It was revenge. It was in my dream again, and it told me...," she paused, unable to go on.

"What did it tell you?" Keaton urged, rubbing circles into her back. It felt like something her mom would do, and she teared up.

"It told me the truth. That I was a human waste of space and that you two would be better off without me."

"Oh, sweetheart," Frankie whispered, voice sadder than Carsen had ever heard it. It made her feel worse, the knowledge that she had caused that hurt, and she started to cry in earnest.

"I'm sorry! I'm sorry. All I do is ruin things. I almost hoped that the faerie would change me, fix me. So I could be better, perfect even. That's all I wanted. I never wanted to hurt you. I'm so sorry."

"You're perfect now. There's no other way to say it. We love you, Carsen. Both of us. And there's nothing you could do to 'improve' yourself," he said, pale fingers using air quotes, "that would make us somehow love you more."

269

The speech was so genuine that Carsen couldn't help but believe him. His eyes were aching, lonelier than the ocean in the middle of the night, and she wanted to do something, anything, to make the look on his face go away.

33

Strawberry / You're Losing Me

Carsen awoke the next morning to find that Frankie had singlehandedly dug a swimming hole. She stumbled out into the front yard to examine it, stuck between starstruck and irritated at the sheer able-bodiedness of the act.

"It's nine in the morning. When did you have time to do this?" Carsen asked in stunned admiration.

"I'm an early riser," Frankie said easily. She practically skipped on her way back to the house.

The girls were giggling madly, splashing about, high on the finest things of life. She looked back to the porch, where Keaton and Frankie were now locked in conversation. Keaton was sat far back in the shadows, careful to stay away from the edge of the porch and the rays of sun that were edging their way across the wood paneling. Frankie, on the other hand, stood near the edge, her figure silhouetted by sunlight. They

271

were beautiful, and they were hers. Carsen adjusted her hips back into place and leaped into the water.

Life was lovely.

–

After several hours of swimming, with Keaton chasing everybody around with 65 SPF sunscreen at regular intervals, the girls trounced inside to dry off. Carsen found Frankie waiting for her, holding a flannel that was three sizes too big for both of them.

"Something I found in college at a Goodwill.[37] I was a big thrifter back when I lived in the city."

"Oh!" Carsen exclaimed, pleasantly surprised. She and Frankie had never discussed education before. "What did you study?" she asked, not sure what she expected.

She blushed a bit. "Theoretical physics."

Carsen laughed.

"What?" Frankie demanded defensively.

"You! You're just so…impossibly excellent. You're incredibly kind, a great cook, apparently a genius, and very hot. Did I mention very hot? *Very* hot."

Frankie examined her closely, one long dark arm over the back of the couch in a way that made Carsen feel like she was

272

in an old movie and about to be kissed.

"What?" Carsen asked nervously. Even after all this time, Frankie still gave her that flood of jitters in her stomach.

"You," she said.

She had been right about the kiss. Frankie leaned in and let her honey lips dance with hers.

Carsen sighed dreamily.

Life was perfect.

—

It turned out that life had been too perfect. It all came apart after dinner, a night in August that she would never forget.

"Carsen, could I speak with you privately?" Atticus asked, eyes not quite meeting hers.

Keaton's brow furrowed, and he visibly stiffened, drawing himself up. "Anything you need to say to Carsen, you can say in front of us, too." He looked hesitantly towards her as he said this, as though worried that he had overstepped.

Carsen gave him a shy smile, then turned to Atticus. "You can say it here."

Atticus smiled sadly and nodded his agreement. Carsen didn't like the way he was nervously wringing his hands.

"I've researched it from every angle. I even corresponded with my friends from the University of Edinburgh. There's no fixing you, Carsen. I'm sorry. The cure would be worse than the disease."

Carsen felt her body sag under the weight of hearing what she had always known deep down. She could dimly hear Keaton and Frankie's raised voices but couldn't make out a word. All she could hear was her heart beating in her ears.

"I'll be in my room," she said roughly. She rose, swaying a bit, and Keaton's cold fingers encircled her arms, steadying her.

"Are you sure? I don't think you should be alone right now," Frankie worried.

Keaton was stroking her face, cold fingers cooling her hot cheeks. She thought she might faint. She was going to lose them, everything she had always known and been in perpetual fear of since she arrived.

"I just need a second to gather myself. I'll be back." She stood again and wavered, feeling the cold on her again.

"Stop," Keaton called. He was holding her hand.

Keaton insisted on guiding her to the bathroom, hands a frozen vice grip. His face was even paler than usual - for some reason, this had hit him nearly as hard as it had her.

You know, she thought. *You're losing me.*[38]

"I'll be right here," he said.

She gazed at his watercolor eyes. "I know."

–

Carsen stared at herself in the mirror. Her face was gray.[39] It was the face of someone who would always be in pain, always be a burden. Tears streaked her cheeks, but she hadn't felt them start and certainly didn't know how to stop them. She could feel the self she had become fading.

She knew what she had to do.

It's time.[40]

She couldn't bear to look at Keaton as they returned to the kitchen, opting to just hold his hand in silence as they walked.

Atticus stood as she came in and opened his mouth to say something. This time, she interrupted him.

"Atticus, I appreciate all you have done for me, more than I can tell you. You gave me a hope I haven't had in years. I know you did everything possible. Would you mind letting me speak to Frankie and Keaton alone for a moment?"

He nodded and left the room in a rush, heading towards the stairs.

She turned to the loves of her life, dreading what was to come.

275

"I thought a cure would come through in time. But now that I know it won't[41]... I have to go."

"I don't understand," Frankie said slowly.

"I know you don't.[42]" Carsen thought her chest would burst open with the hurt.

"I do." Keaton sounded...angry? She looked at him to find that furious flash in his eyes. It had been a while since it had been directed at her.

"You think this changes anything? I know you, Carsen. I know you think you only deserve us whole or some foolishness like that. It's not true, not at all."

"It's only going to get worse, Keaton. I will get worse. And I will hurt, and you both will have to watch. And I don't want that for you. I don't want it for me, either."

"Wait here." Keaton stood suddenly and, without another word, was running down the hallway.[43]

Carsen returned her attention to Frankie to find her crying silently. Swallowing bile, sickened by herself, she reached out and tried to hold her hand. Frankie wouldn't hold it back.

Keaton returned, panting slightly. He must not have had his blood for the week yet.

"I've been saving this for the right time. Now has to be it, I suppose." He opened his hand to reveal a matching pair of rings. They were beautiful, intricate silver detailing with a small diamond capping it off. Frankie gasped. Carsen felt time stop.

"They're promise rings. I sent out for them to be made based on how I remembered my mother's ring. I wanted to... promise myself to both of you. For however long we have. I had hoped it would be more time than this, but if you insist on going back to Massachusetts, you should have it now. Give me your hand."

He had forced the anger down for this moment, and when he took her hand, it was gentle. He slipped a ring onto her finger first, eyes transfixed by her hands. He turned to Frankie next, all sad smiles as he kissed her tears away before slipping her ring on.

Carsen was frozen, thinking about forever and all the meanings it could have. Why would anyone want her forever? Why would anyone cry over her? How could she do this to her two monsters, people she loved more than she had ever loved anyone?

She thought suddenly of the way that she felt when Frankie transformed. The pain Carsen felt at the pain her werewolf felt. An agony, yes, but bearable for what came after. The post-change cuddles, the warm tea, and the being the one who got to be there for her.

It occurred to her then that they might feel that way. That

277

they might enjoy being the ones who were there for her. It had never crossed her mind before; she so despised the thought of being seen in that way, it had never occurred to her to think that of that vulnerability, a sort of gift.

"Carsen?" Keaton prompted.

Abruptly, she realized she'd been quiet too long. She looked up from her lap. Frankie was still crying, eyes puffy, nose swollen. Carsen's heart ached. She looked at Keaton, stilled by the stone of his expression.

"Can you bear it? The weight of the watching?" she asked quietly.

Keaton's affirmative nod shook the earth beneath her. She turned to Frankie, praying for the first time in her life.

Frankie's voice was an open wound. "For you, of course."

Carsen broke completely then, sobbing harder than she ever had before.

She didn't need to break her own heart. The details were gravy.

34

I Always Knew

"Franks, I love you, but I'm sweating to death." Carsen grumbled, rolling away from the woman.

Keaton scoffed. "I'm not, stay here." He nudged his way even deeper into the crook of Frances's shoulder.

The three were sprawled out in their tri-bed, as they had taken to calling it. They had co-opted Frankie's room, which had the layout to make it possible, and had shoved all three of their beds together to make a gigantic one for them all to share. It had worked surprisingly well, and although shutting Frankie's door now took some finesse, it was well worth it for the memories that they were making every night.

"Keaton!" Atticus's voice came from across the house. The blond man shoved his head underneath the pillows and groaned.

"*Keaton!*" The voice was more insistent this time, and Frankie and Carsen, in silent agreement, started poking at the man's ribcage.

"You two are the worst," he groused.

Keaton rolled up off the bed and grumbling, stumbled towards the sound, leaving the two of them curled into one another, hot breath brushing across bare skin.

"When did you know? That you loved me?" Carsen asked, gazing wonderingly at her, with her chocolate eyes that melted in the light and the dark skin that shimmered in the sun.

"I always knew,"[44] she said simply. "I knew the second that I saw you. The moment I laid eyes on you when you were floating that trunk across the lawn, I knew I would love you forever."

–

It was a warm day, the sun soaking the skin of those who were equipped for UV rays. Keaton and Atticus sat next to them, huge floppy hats hiding their faces and necks and gloves, long sleeves, and jeans on to cover any possible exposed skin. Atticus wore fine leather driving gloves, befitting his elegant demeanor.

Fiona's birthday party was in full swing, with balloons as far as the eye could see and a cake bigger than the girl herself.

Carsen drew an envelope out of the front pocket of her

overalls and lifted it to her mouth. She kissed it gently and whispered into its fold. Then she raised it into the air and asked the wind to take it where it needed to go. The wind obliged, whistling merrily as it whisked it away. It fluttered a bit as it went, waving a little goodbye.

"What did you tell it?" Keaton asked, eyes steady on her. Frankie stroked her arm comfortingly, mouth halfway smiling.

Carsen knew they both already knew the answer - supernatural hearing will do that - but she answered anyway.

"I love you."

V

Epilogue

35

Two Birds

Mom,
I won't be coming back. I'm sure you gathered that when my name faded from the bookshelf. I fell in love. Twice, actually. Who would've thought?

I wanted you to know that there is another little girl who stirs her potions counterclockwise because it gives them that extra kick. She also sleeps with rose quartz under her pillow and does a maypole ceremony even though there's no magickal reason for it, just for fun. Every day that I taught Maddie, I remembered the way you taught me my magick. And the more she learned, the more I saw you in the way she did things. I wonder if you felt this way when you taught me. I wonder if girlhood is just a becoming of every woman who's ever been. I wonder if someday there will be another girl who doesn't know our names but still makes her tea with mulberry when she wants to see what's to come.

I know you won't understand why I've chosen to stay, and I know that's exactly why I have to. I miss you every day. I know you miss me, too. I also know that if I came home, I'd regret it forever.

Take care of yourself for me. Please don't worry about me, I'm happy. I'm so happy, Mom.

I love you.

Carsen

P.S. -

When you open the shop tomorrow, go into the basement storeroom . There's a stack of letters under the third floor-board to the right of the valerian root. You can read them. They're for you, after all. They're all the things I ever wanted to say to you but was too scared to. I'm ready for you to hear them now.

36

Lyrical Key

Hidden in many of these chapters are quotes or inspired by quotes from the songs that each chapter is respectively named for. See if you found them all!

Autumn

Chapter Two -

Song: *To Watch the World Spin Without You* (Mon Rovîa)

Lyric: "Every rose has its thorns, I guess"

Chapter Three -

Song: *treehouse* (kelseydog)

Lyric: "Do not enter is written on the doorway"

Chapter Four -

Song: *Interlude: I'm Not Angry Anymore* (Paramore)

Lyric: "I don't think badly of you"

Chapter Five -

Song: *Haunted (Taylor's Version)* (Taylor Swift)

Lyric: "A fragile line"

Chapter Six -

Song: *Sparks Fly (Taylor's Version)* (Taylor Swift)

Lyric: "A full on rainstorm"

Chapter Seven -

Song: *i heard you were looking like the moon* (Richard Orofino)

Lyric: "I hope you're feeling a little bit better"

Chapter Eight -

Song: *Razorblade* (Richard Orofino)

Lyric: "please don't close your eyes," "Razorblade pressed against my vein," "I'm sorry I don't always know what's best"

Chapter Nine -

Song: *Satellite Heart* (Anya Marina)

Lyric: "You know, I haven't slept in weeks"

Winter

Chapter One -

Song: *Tenenbaum* (The Paper Kites)

Lyric: "You're a bitter kind...Sour... Rough kind of a day"

Chapter Two -

Song: *Motion Sickness* (Phoebe Bridgers)

Lyric: "I miss you like a little kid"

Chapter Three -

Song: *It's Alright* (Mother Mother)

289

Lyric: "Not a monster"

Chapter Four

Song: *Keep Yourself Warm* (Frightened Rabbit)

Lyric: "Can you see in the dark"

Chapter Five

Song: *Just a Little While* (the 502s)

Lyric: "my life was thin"

Chapter Six

Song: *She* (Dodie)

Lyric: "Smells like lemongrass"

Chapter Seven

Song: *Loverboy* (A Wall)

Lyric: "the way you're looking at me"

Spring

Chapter Three

Song: *Coastline* (Hollow Coves)

Lyric: "feels like we're in a dream"

Chapter Four

Song: *Seven* (Taylor Swift)

Lyric: "I hit my peak at seven"

Chapter Five:

Song: *Invisible String* (Taylor Swift)

Lyric: "Invisible string"

Song: *Shrike* (Hozier)

Lyric: "singing like a bird about it now"

Chapter Six

Song: *Witches* (Alice Phoebe Lou)

291

Lyric: "moon lit eyes"

Chapter Seven

Song: *Where's My Love* (SYML)

Lyric: "just come home"

Chapter Eight

Song: *Heat Waves - Stripped Back* (Glass Animals)

Lyric: "you need something I could never give"

Chapter Nine

Song: *The Archer* (Taylor Swift)

Lyric: "they see right through me, can you see right through me, I see right through me"

Summer

Chapter One

Song: *Boreas* (The Oh Hellos)

Lyric: "Be a bit of warmth for you", "cold linoleum"

Chapter Two

Song: *August (Acoustic)* (flipturn)

Lyric: "We don't have the time"

Chapter Three

Song: *Rises the Moon* (Liana Flores)

Lyric: "Breathe, breathe, breathe"

Chapter Four

Song: *Achilles, Come Down* (Gang of Youths)

Lyric: "can you hear me", "come down", "end it all now, it's a pointless resistance for you"

Chapter Five

Song: *Strawberry* (Andrew Montana)

Lyric: "something i found in college"

Chapter Five

Song: *You're Losing Me (From the Vault)* (Taylor Swift)

Lyric: "i don't understand, i know you don't", "we thought a cure would come", "it's time", "my face was gray", "running down the hallway", "fading"

Chapter Six

Song: *I Always Knew* (The Vaccines)

Lyric: "I always knew"

Afterword

I came up with this idea while I had COVID-19 alone in another country at Christmas time. I was living in Scotland at the time, in a teensy flat all by myself. It *had* been going great until I got seriously sick all alone and totally quarantined for ten days. I spent a lot of time watching and reading the *Twilight* series and feeling sorry for myself.

As someone who grew up immersed in Tumblr culture and the "why not both" meme, my thoughts naturally went there as I watched Edward, Jacob, and Bella ignore the blatant sexual tension between all three of them. This book is about that, and about being a young girl afraid of losing who you were to womanhood, about being disabled and feeling profoundly unlovable because of it. I wrote this for the girl and the boy I fell in love with when I was in high school. I wrote this for a sixteen-year-old me who wanted to know what it was like to be loved so badly that sometimes it was all she could think about. I wrote this to see myself in a love story. I hope you see yourself too.

I've been trying to tell this story since I was a kid. It is all the moments I've lived, and all the ones I hope are coming. I hope I did them justice.

Acknowledgements

to my mother, my singular constant - sorry you had to read your daughter's attempts at writing sex scenes.

to taylor swift, for teaching me everything that i know about love.

to nicole, for your editing finesse, and for the psychic link that we share.

to effie, for being my home in a place that was anything but.

to jen, for your taste in books, being my biggest cheerleader, and for sending all my favorite voice notes.

to alexus massenburg. thank you for bringing my story to life - i can't thank you enough for your beautiful art. PLEASE check out alexus's art @aleuborealis on twitter.

* * *

Notes

TO WATCH THE WORLD SPIN AROUND

1   'To Watch the World Spin Without You', Mon Rovîa

TREEHOUSE

2   'Treehouse', kelseydog

INTERLUDE: I'M NOT ANGRY ANYMORE

3   'Interlude: I'm Not Angry Anymore', Paramore

HAUNTED

4   'Haunted (Taylor's Version)', Taylor Swift

SPARKS FLY

5   'Sparks Fly (Taylor's Version)', Taylor Swift

I HEARD YOU WERE LOOKING LIKE THE MOON

6   'I heard you were looking like the moon', Richard Orofino

RAZORBLADE

7   'Razorblade', Richard Orofino

8   'Razorblade', Richard Orofino

9   'Razorblade', Richard Orofino

SATELLITE HEART

10 'Satellite Heart', Anya Marina

TENENBAUM

11 'Tenenbaum', The Paper Kites

12 'Tenenbaum', The Paper Kites

MOTION SICKNESS

IT'S ALRIGHT

KEEP YOURSELF WARM

JUST A LITTLE WHILE

SHE

LOVERBOY

COASTLINE

SEVEN

INVISIBLE STRING / SHRIKE

WITCHES

WHERE'S MY LOVE

HEAT WAVES - STRIPPED BACK

About the Author

Due to listening to too much Taylor Swift as a child, Katherine believes every story anyone ever tells is about romance. She integrates love into all of her work, from her nonfiction pieces to her poetry collection to her various novels. A librarian by day and an author by night, these days she writes romance and fantasy novels, sometimes both at the same time. She spends most of her time having conversations about love and our incredible magical capacity for it.

You can connect with me on:
🌏 https://ananxiouslibrarian.com
🔗 https://www.youtube.com/channel/UC3bxj9Wv4Pwb623u_uMqdGw

Subscribe to my newsletter:
✉ http://eepurl.com/iubRqU

Also by Katherine Watson

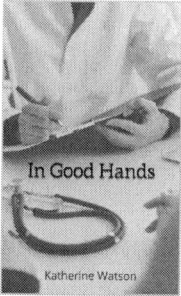

In Good Hands
Georgia Levinson just wants to feel better. Or at least well enough to get through her classes. She's been exhausted for years, but every doctor she's ever seen has told her it's because she's overweight. Hopefully this (very cute) doctor at the school clinic will be different.

Teddy Diaz loves being a doctor. Sure, his residency advisor is an egomaniac and he's sometimes not great with a needle, but he cares about people and wants to do it for the rest of his life. Which is why a certain blonde needs to get out of his head so he can not get thrown out of his program for unprofessional conduct.

Once and Forever

High school romances can be tricky. Especially when you're a boy with a crush on the new boy in school, who looks and acts an awful lot like King Arthur. Especially when your friend groups looks a lot like the Knights of the Round Table, and maybe you've been here before. Merlin seems to be living the same love affair again and again, but that's not possible. Is it?

In this compelling and original YA story, chock full of magical realism, slow-burning love, and gay high schoolers, it just might be.

Manufactured by Amazon.ca
Bolton, ON

37803794R00173